SUPER SLUGGER

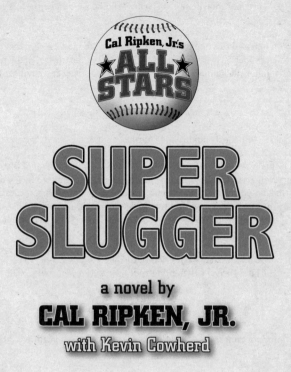

SUPER SLUGGER

a novel by

CAL RIPKEN, JR.

with Kevin Cowherd

𝒟𝒾𝓈𝓃𝑒𝓎 • Hyperion

Los Angeles New York

A special thanks to Stephanie Owens Lurie, Editorial Director of
Disney • Hyperion Books, for her incomparable guidance and boundless
patience and good humor. All writers should have an editor this good.
—K. C.

Previously published in hardcover as *Super-Sized Slugger*

First Disney • Hyperion Hardcover edition, March 2012
First Disney • Hyperion Paperback edition, February 2013
10 9 8 7 6 5 4 3 2
V475-2873-0-15110
Printed in the United States of America

Library of Congress Control Number for the Hardcover Edition: 2012043426

Ripken, Cal, 1960–
 [Super-sized slugger]
 Super slugger : a novel / Cal Ripken, Jr. ; with Kevin Cowherd.—1st Disney
Hyperion paperback edition.
    pages cm
 Originally published in 2012 under title: Super-sized slugger.
 Summary: Thirteen-year-old Cody Parker moves to Baltimore, Maryland,
where as a fat eighth-grader, he has to deal with brutal teasing from a baseball
teammate, and his school is beset by a rash of mysterious thefts that threaten to
sideline Cody and ruin a golden season for his team.
 ISBN 978-1-4231-4004-7
[1. Baseball—Fiction. 2. Moving, Household—Fiction. 3. Overweight persons—
Fiction. 4. Bullies—Fiction. 5. Stealing—Fiction. 6. Schools—Fiction. 7. Middle
schools—Fiction. 8. Baltimore (Md.)—Fiction. 9. Mystery and detective stories.]
I. Cowherd, Kevin. II. Title.
 PZ7.R4842Sv 2013
 [Fic]—dc23   2012043426

SUSTAINABLE
FORESTRY
INITIATIVE

Certified Chain of Custody
Promoting Sustainable Forestry

www.sfiprogram.org
SFI-01054

The SFI label applies to the text stock

Visit www.DisneyBooks.com

To Maura and Bill, and Stephen and Anne.
Thanks for everything.
—Kevin Cowherd

Cal Ripken, Jr.'s
★ ALL ★
STARS

SUPER SLUGGER

Cody braced himself for the usual reaction. It was the first day of practice for the Orioles of the Dulaney Babe Ruth League, and Coach Ray Hammond was going down the line, asking each kid to say his name and the position he wanted to play.

"Cody Parker. Third base," he said when it was his turn.

From somewhere behind him, he heard snickers.

Here we go, he thought.

"Third base, eh?" Coach Hammond said. He studied Cody for a moment.

Cody knew what was coming next. Coach would try to break it to him gently. *Why not try the outfield, son? You're a little, um,* big *for third base. In fact, I'm thinking right field would be perfect for you.*

Everyone knew the unspoken rule: right field was for fat guys. And slow guys. And guys with thick glasses and big ears and bad haircuts. If you smacked of dorkiness at all, or if you looked the least bit unathletic, they stuck you in right field, baseball's equivalent of the slow class. Then they got down on their knees and prayed to the baseball gods that no one would ever hit a ball your way in a real game.

That's why Cody hated right field. Hated it almost as much as he hated his new life here in Dullsville, Maryland, also known as Baltimore, where the major league team stunk and people talked funny, saying "WARSH-ington" instead of "Washington" and "POH-leece" instead of "police."

No thanks, he thought. Give me Wisconsin, any day.

Immediately he felt a stab of homesickness as he thought about his old house on leafy Otter Trail. He pictured his corner bedroom on the second floor with the wall-to-wall Milwaukee Brewers posters, especially the giant one of his hero, Prince Fielder, following through on a mighty swing to hit another majestic home run. He saw the big tree house in his backyard, and the basketball hoop over the garage, and the trails in the nearby woods, where he used to—

"Cody?" Coach was saying now.

Cody shook his head and refocused.

"Okay," Coach said. "Let's see how you do at third."

Hallelujah! For an instant, Cody thought of giving Coach a big hug. But Coach didn't seem like the hugging type. He was a big man with a short, no-nonsense crew cut and an old-fashioned walrus mustache. He looked more like the hearty-handshake type. Except his hearty handshake could probably crush walnuts.

Minutes later, the Orioles broke into groups for infield practice. Trotting out to third base, Cody was surprised to see he was the only one trying out for the position.

Then he heard the sound of heavy footsteps behind him and felt a sharp elbow in the ribs.

"Out of the way, fat boy," a voice growled.

Wonderful, Cody thought. The welcoming committee is here. Looking up, he saw a tall, broad-shouldered boy he recognized as Dante Rizzo.

"Instead of 'fat,' could we agree on *burly*?" Cody said, smiling.

That's it, turn on the charm, he thought. Kill 'em with laughter.

"Shut up and stay out of my way," Dante said, spitting into his glove and scowling.

So much for trying the charm, Cody thought. But the truth was, he *didn't* consider himself fat—not in your classic Doritos-scarfing, Big Mac–inhaling, look-at-the-butt-on-this-kid sort of way.

His mother said he was big-boned. It was his dad who called him burly. To Cody, burly was preferable to big-boned, which sounded like he had some kind of freak skeletal disorder. Cody thought he was built along the lines of the great Prince Fielder, if you could picture the Brewers' first baseman as a thirteen-year-old with a thick mop of red hair and freckles.

Big, sure. Even chunky. But nothing that made you wrinkle your nose and go, "Ewww."

On the other hand, Dante obviously didn't share this assessment of Cody's body type, which came as no great surprise. Cody thought back to the first time he had met Dante—although *met* might not be the right word—on his first day at his new school, York Middle.

Cody had been eating lunch, sitting in the back of the cafeteria with a few other kids, mostly nerds and misfits who seemed just as lonely as he was. Suddenly, something warm and moist smacked him in the back of the neck. It turned out to be a soggy pizza crust.

Whipping around, Cody had seen a tall boy with long dark hair smirking at him and nudging his buddies.

"Congratulations," the kid sitting next to Cody had said. "You've just been introduced to Dante the Terrible."

"Yeah," another kid had added. "He's in eighth grade and he's fifteen—draw your own conclusions. His hobby is pounding people. And if you mess with him, he's got two older brothers who'll mess with *you*."

"Vincent and Nick. We call them the Rottweiler Twins," a third kid had chimed in. "On account of they're so warm and cuddly."

Remembering the pizza incident now, Cody shot a nervous glance at Dante. Just my luck he plays baseball too, Cody thought. Why can't he play lacrosse like every other kid in Maryland?

And what are the odds we'd both end up on the Orioles? And be trying out for the same position?

About the same as the odds of me being confused with Prince Fielder, he decided.

Coach picked up his black fungo bat to begin hitting ground balls to the third basemen, and Dante elbowed Cody aside.

"Back of the line, rookie," he said. "Veterans go first."

"My boyish good looks don't count?" Cody said.

At this, the rest of the infielders covered their mouths with their gloves to hide their smiles. Cody wasn't sure whether they were laughing *with* him or *at* him.

Dante glared and shook his fist. "I thought I told you to shut up," he growled.

Great, Cody thought. I'm the new kid. I'm a little out of shape. And now the local thug wants to use me like a piñata.

Maybe this was Dante's second year with the Orioles, and maybe he had played third base last year, but he was an awkward infielder, anyone could see that. He was a good two inches taller than Cody, yet he crouched way too low and took short, clumsy strides to each grounder, bobbling the first two. As a big guy himself, Cody sometimes felt he had all the mobility of the Washington Monument. But he knew the key was to take advantage of your height and strength to cross over and move laterally.

One weekend last year, in fact, he had watched YouTube videos of every big third baseman in the major leagues, just to see how they set up and moved to a ground ball. "How come you don't study this hard for science class?" his dad had asked. And the short answer was simple: it wasn't baseball. Nothing in the world got Cody excited like baseball.

The other thing Cody noticed was that Dante's throws to first base tended to sail. This was because he never set his feet properly. Only a couple of great leaping grabs by the first baseman—a rangy kid with terrific hands—saved the throws from going over the fence.

After botching yet another grounder, Dante slammed his glove to the ground and cursed loudly.

"Language!" Coach yelled, shooting Dante a look. "We had this problem last year." Dante kicked angrily at the dirt and muttered under his breath. A couple of players shook their heads.

"All right, Cody," Coach said. "Your turn."

"Don't let the pressure get to you, lard-butt," Dante whispered.

"Remember: I'm *burly*," Cody whispered back, earning another death stare. "I thought we went over this."

Now Cody sensed that all eyes were on him, the way they always were whenever he had to prove himself on a new team. It was always: *Let's see what the big guy's got— probably nothing.*

He dropped easily into his crouch, weight balanced evenly on the balls of his feet, body tilted slightly forward to get a jump on the ball. He punched the pocket of his glove and straightened the brim of his cap, at the same time marveling at how relaxed he felt.

This was what he loved about baseball: how comfortable he always felt when he stepped across the white lines. Everywhere else he felt like a dork—a *giant* dork—most of the time. But never on a baseball diamond.

"You're always smiling when you play ball," his mom had said once. And why not? Cody thought. Baseball's easy. It's the other stuff in life that gets complicated.

He gobbled up the first four grounders hit to him and made strong throws to first each time, earning a nod from Coach. But Cody could tell he was about to be tested. They always think it's a fluke when the big guy looks good, he thought.

Sure enough, the next ball was a scorching two-hopper to his right. He dove and snared the ball backhanded at the last second, kicking up a cloud of dirt. Quickly, he scrambled to his feet and fired a bullet to first.

"Not bad!" Coach yelled. "Almost made that look easy!"

The last ball was another shot, this time to Cody's left, in the hole between shortstop and third. He took three quick steps, lunged for the ball, and spun 180 degrees before whipping a strong throw to first.

The kid at first nodded and pointed his glove at Cody, as if to say: *You da man!*

"Hey!" Coach said, grinning now. "That's a big-league play right there!"

"You got lucky, fat boy," Dante muttered from a few feet away as Coach moved on to hit grounders to the shortstop. "No way you're that good."

Cody shrugged and said nothing. That was the other thing he loved about baseball: the chance to prove people wrong, make them shut up. He'd been playing the game since he was, what, six years old? How many times had kids made fun of his weight, then stared slack-jawed when he backhanded a hard shot at third or legged out a double with a headfirst slide? The name-calling tended to stop pretty quickly after that.

Besides, he thought, the big leagues were full of terrific players who didn't exactly look like they lived on salad and granola bars. David "Big Papi" Ortiz with the Boston Red Sox. C. C. Sabathia with the New York Yankees. Pablo Sandoval with the San Francisco Giants. Adam Dunn with the Chicago White Sox. There was a time when fans might have blamed steroids. Now players just seemed to be bigger and stronger, and a lot of that came from their work in the weight room.

After hitting balls to everyone, Coach announced that it was time for batting practice. He grabbed his glove and a bucketful of balls and headed for the pitcher's mound.

"Everyone gets ten swings," he said. "Make 'em count, boys."

Hearing this, Cody pumped his fist and thought, *Yessss!* He loved playing third base, but hitting was his favorite part of the game. He could have had a bad day at school, his mom and dad could be on him about his messy room, his mind could be buzzing with a hundred different thoughts, but as soon as he stepped into the batter's box, he felt calm and focused. It was an amazing transformation—maybe not as dramatic as what Spider-Man or Thor went through when they went from supergeek to superhero, but close.

The Orioles broke into hitting groups. Right away, everyone saw that Coach was throwing some serious heat. He was pitching from a full windup, and even though his control was good, the ball was whistling as it smacked into the backstop.

Cody noticed that few of his teammates seemed eager to dig in.

"Hey, ease up, Coach!" Dante yelled when it was his turn. "Let the big dog hunt!"

"You guys want me to throw underhand?" Coach said in a mocking voice. "Maybe we can get the Braves to throw underhand for the season opener too."

Cody shagged balls in the outfield until Coach finally waved him in to hit with the last group.

Right before he was up, Cody unzipped his equipment bag and pulled out his bat. Then he carefully wiped it down with a towel. Just looking at the bat made him smile. It was a beauty, all right: silver with red flecks, a thirty-one-inch, twenty-one-ounce birthday present from his mom and dad. If you held it at just the right angle, with the sun glinting off it, it looked like a flaming sword as you walked to the plate.

He gripped the bat, brought the barrel to his lips, and glanced around to see if anyone was looking. Then he whispered, "Time to go to work, buddy."

He wasn't sure when he first took to talking to his bat—it had been a couple of years now. He guessed he did it for good luck—not that the bat always listened to him. And he probably did it to calm himself down at the plate too, and help him focus. But this little ritual wasn't something he wanted to share with his new teammates just yet.

He could imagine the reaction: *So you talk to your bat, huh, Parker? And what does Mr. Bat say back? Does he tell you to lay off the high fastball? Or: don't swing at anything in the dirt?*

That's all I need, Cody thought. People thinking I'm fat *and* crazy.

As he dug in against Coach and took a couple of warm-up swings, he stole a glance at the short left-field fence. It looked so inviting for a right-handed hitter, like there was a big neon sign out there flashing the message: HIT IT HERE! Forget the fence, he told himself. Start trying to jack home runs to impress Coach and you'll mess up your swing, big-time.

Instead he focused on the mantra his dad had preached for years: "Short, level swing. Just hit the ball somewhere— and hit it hard."

As it had so many other times, the advice paid off. Cody roped the first three pitches for what would have been clean singles and followed that by driving two balls into the gap in left-center field. On the sixth pitch, as often hap-pened when he was swinging well, he smashed a long, soaring drive that cleared the fence in left field by ten feet.

Now Cody heard excited murmurs from the Orioles ringed around the backstop behind him.

"Whoa!" one kid said. "Tagged!"

"Big kid has game!" another voice said.

You like that? Cody said to himself. Watch this!

But this time he swung too hard at the next pitch, swung from his heels, missed it completely, and almost fell down, the way Prince did sometimes. Then the big man would climb back in the batter's box and flash a sheepish grin that seemed to say *Kids, don't try that at home*.

"Felt the breeze back here, dude," a third kid said as the others chuckled.

Relax, Cody told himself. Don't lunge at it. Wait for it. And this time he turned on the pitch perfectly, smacking another shot that easily cleared the fence in left. Now the murmurs grew even louder.

After he whipped around to see where the ball landed, Coach let out a whoop.

"Boy has some thunder in his bat, doesn't he?"

Big kid comes through, Cody thought, more relieved than anything.

When practice was over, Cody was tired and hungry. But he was pleased with how he'd done the first day with his new team. As he walked off the field, the lanky kid who had made the great plays at first base tapped him on the shoulder.

"You're the new kid, right?" he said. "I'm Jordy Marsh. You looked pretty good out there."

"Thanks," Cody said. "You looked pretty good yourself. Way to get up for those high throws."

Jordy smiled and leaped in the air, pretending to throw down a ferocious dunk. "Yeah, I'm a regular Kobe Bryant when I have to be," he said.

Now they were joined by another boy. Cody recognized him as the brown-haired kid who had taken most of the balls at shortstop, effortlessly vacuuming up one hard shot after another.

"Connor Sullivan," the kid said, giving Cody a fist bump. "Boy, you were killin' it in practice today."

Cody looked down and scratched idly at the dirt with his spikes, searching for something to say.

"Coach was probably taking it easy on me," he said finally.

"No way," Connor said. "Coach wouldn't take it easy on his own grandmother. You were dialed in, dude."

Jordy and Connor jogged off, saying they'd see him in school the next day.

Seconds later, Dante ran by and jabbed another elbow into Cody's ribs.

"Do yourself a favor, fat boy!" he shouted over his shoulder. "Find another position!"

Terrific, Cody thought. Eleven other kids on this team, and I have to play the same position as the budding middle school hit man. Who is definitely not happy now that I showed him up.

Cody changed out of his spikes, gathered up his bat and glove, and began the long walk to the parking lot, where his mom would be waiting in her car.

The late April sun was setting. The tall pine trees that ringed Eddie Murray Field cast long shadows everywhere. He shivered slightly in the damp air.

He had a feeling he'd be seeing a lot of Dante Rizzo from now on.

Which might not necessarily be a good thing.

"Chunkster?"

"Yeah, I get that one a lot."

"Tubby?"

"No, that's old school."

"Fat boy?"

"Yep. One of my new, uh, admirers loves that one."

"Tub of goo?"

"*Mo-mmm!*"

"Sorry, sweetie. Just kidding. It's just that Letterman once called someone that on his TV show. Terry Forster. A pitcher for the Atlanta Braves."

"Well, no one's called me that yet. Don't give them any ideas."

"Don't worry, they won't."

Cody and his mom were at the kitchen table in their new house on Bosley Road, the sun streaming through the bay windows on a warm Saturday morning. They were just sitting down to a breakfast of orange juice, sausages, and blueberry pancakes, which Cody drowned in a puddle of maple syrup.

Cody's dad, a detective with the Baltimore Police Department, had just left for work, pulling on his jacket and grabbing his laptop as he dashed out the door. As usual, the sight of the gun and holster on his hip made Cody's mom wince. Even after all these years, she hated being reminded of the dangers of police work.

Maybe that was why she tried to turn everything into a joke, to help her forget the scary stuff. She was listing all the names overweight kids get called. It seemed like there were dozens, maybe even hundreds. Cody figured he'd heard just about all of them—quite a few recently, in fact. It turned out mean kids weren't any more creative in Maryland than they were in Wisconsin.

"The point is, they're just words," his mom said. "Sure, they can be hurtful. But only if you let them."

"I know," Cody said. "But being the new kid is hard enough. When you're heavy too, and the other kids are calling you names like Cody *Porker*..."

Kate Parker sighed and shook her head. "You're right, dear. I'm sure it's not easy. But the names will stop, once they get to know you. For now, try to ignore it."

Cody was quiet for a moment, staring down at his plate.

"I miss our old house," he said finally. "And my friends back home."

"I know you do," his mom said. She reached across the table, squeezed his hand, and smiled softly. "But this is your home now. Your dad had a job offer he couldn't pass up. And you'll make a ton of new friends. You're smart, you're funny, you're athletic—"

"And fat," Cody said morosely. "Kids in school remind me of that every day."

"Uh-uh, no feeling sorry for yourself," his mom said. "You have too much going for you. And you won't be big forever. That baby fat will come off in no time."

"I'm thirteen years old!" Cody said. "How long does baby fat stick around? Until you're thirty?"

His mother smiled again and sipped her coffee. "Listen to Mr. Cheerful," she said, rolling her eyes. "Mr. Upbeat."

For the next few minutes, the two ate in silence. Finally, Cody put down his fork and pushed his plate aside. Today he had eaten just one pancake, instead of his usual two or three, and only one sausage.

He was tired of being the butt of jokes everywhere he went. This morning he had made the decision to start eating healthier and lose weight. He hadn't shared this with his parents yet, although now he saw his mom gaze questioningly at the uneaten pancakes.

Cody stared out the window, lost in thought. For as long as he could remember, he had been bigger than the other kids. It wasn't hard to figure out why. He simply—duh!—ate more. But *why* did he eat more? That part he wasn't so sure about. It almost seemed as if he *needed* more food than other kids.

Instead of having one slice of pizza like everyone else, he'd have two or three. Instead of two chocolate chip cookies, he'd have four. He remembered being shocked at the end-of-the-year cookout at his old school in Milwaukee when, at the end of the meal, all the other kids ran off to play dodgeball. That time he had almost shouted: *Wait, they've got more burgers on the grill! The party's just getting started!*

And maybe his mom and dad were right about the way he scarfed his food. "You eat so fast, your brain doesn't register that you're full," his mom was always saying. Okay, guilty as charged on that one.

It wasn't as if he didn't get any exercise. Baseball was his first love, but he liked dodgeball, basketball, football, and soccer too—anything you played with a ball. And he was pretty good at every sport he ever tried.

Just like in baseball, kids who didn't know him would tease him about being fat. They'd break out names like Wide Load and The Bacon-ater and all the rest. Then they'd watch him kick a soccer ball forty yards downfield, or throw a perfect touchdown pass on a dead run—or what passed for a dead run for a big, lumbering kid—in touch football. And suddenly all the teasing would stop—just like that. Often, the kids who were initially his biggest tormentors ended up becoming his best friends.

Cody was hoping that would happen here in Baltimore too. Sports were always his refuge from taunting. If you were a hefty kid, they were the great equalizer. But he also had to admit he hadn't been playing outdoors as much as usual over the past few months. First he'd been busy getting ready for the big move to a new state. And since the move, he'd been spending a lot of time at the computer, chatting with his friends back in Wisconsin.

"Tell me more about how baseball practice went yesterday," Kate Parker said, standing and clearing the dishes.

Cody's spirits lifted immediately. Except for that

embarrassing whiff when he tried to smash the ball to Mars, he wasn't sure you could have a better first practice—especially with a brand-new team. He had definitely impressed his new Orioles teammates with that second home run, the one that cleared the fence by twenty feet and was probably still rolling somewhere.

His mom gave him a quick sideways glance as she loaded the dishwasher. "Could that be a smile I see on Ol' Stoneface?" she said.

"It was pretty fun," Cody said, nodding. "I like Coach Hammond. And I think he likes how I play. Most of the guys on the team seem nice too."

No point in bringing up Dante, Cody thought. His mom didn't need to hear any of that. She was trying to adjust to their new life here in Baltimore too, working hard to make things easy for Cody and his dad while also getting her home-decorating business up and running.

Besides, maybe the whole thing with Dante and third base would blow over. Maybe Dante would just accept that Cody was the better infielder and be content to play another position.

Yeah, right. Well, a guy could dream. And Cody knew one thing: he was almost as good at dreaming as he was at baseball.

Cody arrived forty-five minutes early for practice. He asked his mom to drop him off at empty Eddie Murray Field so he could jog around the bases and do some stretching to loosen up. Which was true, but it wasn't the whole truth.

As soon as she left, he began pacing the parking lot. Fifteen minutes later, a black Ford pickup with oversized tires and Yosemite Sam BACK OFF! mud flaps pulled in.

The driver's-side door swung open, and out jumped Coach Hammond. He walked back to the bed of the truck and pulled out a canvas bag filled with balls, bats, helmets, and catcher's gear.

Cody took a deep breath and waved.

"Hey there!" Coach said, obviously pleased to see him. "You're here early. Or maybe I'm late. Another exhausting day of crime fighting in America. So many bad guys to lock up, so little time."

Cody had heard that Coach was a Baltimore police officer. He wondered if his dad and Coach had met yet, maybe at a crime scene that they both happened to be working.

Not that Cody's dad would ever say much about it. He rarely talked about his work—probably so as not to upset his wife. Lots of times, it didn't make for great dinnertime conversation. *Honey, pass the roast beef and let me tell you about this guy we found with multiple gunshot wounds today. . . .*

"Coach," Cody said, "I was wondering if—"

"You're playing third base?" Coach said, tossing the equipment bag over his shoulder. "You sure are, son. That was some display of fielding you put on the other day."

Cody nodded and looked down.

Coach chuckled. "Well, that's a first," he said. "Usually when I say that to a kid, he's ready to do cartwheels."

"Coach, I can play other positions too," Cody said. "In fact, outfield might be—"

"Nope, you're our third baseman," Coach cut him off, clapping a beefy hand on Cody's shoulder. "You have a strong, accurate arm. And you're a great hitter too. For a big kid, you move real well out there."

Cody nodded again and forced a smile. I might not be moving too well when a certain tall, cranky teammate hears about this, he thought.

He helped Coach unload the catcher's gear and water bottles from the truck as the rest of the Orioles began to trickle in.

"Cody!" said a kid, holding up a ball. "Warm up with me?"

It was the guy who had done most of the catching the other day, Joey. Soon the two of them were joined by the little second baseman, who introduced himself as Willie. Cody kept looking around for Dante, but the big guy was a no-show so far. Maybe he was blowing off practice, Cody thought. Maybe Dante had even quit the team, ticked at Coach for getting on him about the cursing.

Fifteen minutes later, they heard the squealing of tires and saw a battered green Jeep career into the parking lot with the radio blaring. A scowling older boy was behind the wheel, smoking a cigarette; another boy the same age occupied the passenger seat. The rear door was flung open and a familiar figure jumped out.

"Fellas, fellas, fellas!" he cried. "What's up with the Orioles on this fine afternoon?"

Dante Rizzo was in the house. Those other two guys must be the Rottweiler Twins, Cody thought.

As the rest of the Orioles stared and Coach looked at his watch and shook his head, Dante swaggered onto the field and began stretching.

A boy they called Gabe slapped hands with him and said, "What's going on, D?" But Cody noticed most of the other boys seemed to edge away from Dante. Cody and Joey moved away too. But not before Dante spotted Cody and snickered.

A few minutes later, Coach called the Orioles together.

"Boys, I'm excited about this team," he began. "We have some real talent and a great shot to do well this season if we play sound, fundamental baseball. With focus and the right teamwork, we have a chance to be really special. Now, let's go to work."

For the better part of an hour, they had fielding drills: hitting the cutoff man, reviewing where to position themselves for bunts, throwing down to second base on a steal attempt with runners on first and third, etc. Cody was relieved to see that Coach shuttled Dante between third base and left field for the drills. And the big guy didn't seem too upset about the arrangement. At least he wasn't glaring at Cody and making throat-slashing gestures.

But that'll probably change, once he discovers I'm playing third, Cody thought. At which point my life will be over.

Cody could also see that Coach was right about the Orioles' chances of having a great season. Connor and Jordy were both terrific all-round players. Willie Pitts, the slender second baseman, was by far the fastest kid he had ever seen—Cody couldn't imagine anyone being able to throw him out on the base paths. Joey Zinno was an excellent catcher, with a cannon for an arm.

Dante was a far better left fielder than he was a third baseman, and Yancy Arroyo in center field was so smooth he seemed to glide effortlessly to fly balls. Even Gabe Molina in right field looked like a solid player who was not going to embarrass the Orioles.

The pitching seemed outstanding too—at least what Cody saw of right-hander Robbie Hammond, the coach's son, throwing on the sidelines. Robbie was the Orioles' number one pitcher, and Mike Cutko, the short lefty throwing beside him, was their number two.

The only player Cody couldn't figure out was a skinny, gawky-looking kid who took turns alternating with Gabe in right field. The boy never seemed to stop talking, even when he was chasing fly balls and line drives. He talked to anyone who would listen. And when they stopped listening, he kept yammering anyway.

"C'mon, you're better than that!" the kid yelled at himself after dropping an easy fly ball. When he misjudged a line drive a few minutes later, he cried out, "Get your head in the game, Marty!"

When the team finally took a water break, Cody sidled up to Connor and asked, "What's with the chatty guy in right field?"

Connor grinned and waved over Jordy and Willie.

"Jordy," he said, "give us the scouting report on Marty."

Jordy pretended to pull a notebook from his back pocket and thumb through several pages. "Ah, here it is," he said. "Loopus, Marty. Can't hit. Can't catch. Can't throw."

"Wait, there's been an addition," Willie added, acting like he was reading from his own notes. "Says here the boy's slower than your grandma on the bases too."

The three of them laughed. Cody cringed a little, feeling a sting of embarrassment on Marty's behalf. Cody knew how it felt to have kids judging you all the time.

But then Connor held up his hand. "Marty's actually great to have on our team, 'cause he's always trying to make us laugh," he said. "He's probably the smartest kid in the whole school too. I heard he's never gotten anything but straight *A*'s on his report card—since he was in kindergarten."

"Doesn't help much when we're down in the last inning and need a big hit," Willie said with a grin. "But if we ever go up against the other team in positive and negative integers, Marty's the man!"

Now all of them laughed together as Coach waved them back on the field for batting practice.

For the next forty-five minutes, the Orioles put on a show. It was one of those days when everyone was driving the ball. The whole team seemed totally focused—*scary* focused, actually—at the plate. Even Dante was spraying balls to all parts of the field, although he had a looping, totally unorthodox swing, like a guy hacking his way out of a jungle two-handed with a machete.

Connor, Jordy, and Cody, hitting back-to-back-to-back, were outstanding. Each ripped the ball hard on every swing, and each sent two balls soaring over the outfield fence. As Cody's final blast cleared the left-field fence and came to rest near the concession stand, the Orioles who were shagging balls in the outfield began bowing and chanting: "We're not worthy! We're not worthy!"

"Six bombs by three different guys!" Willie shouted. "Coach, you might as well tell the league to give us the trophy right now!"

On the mound, Coach nodded and grinned. He took off his cap and wiped the sweat from his forehead.

"Something's going on!" he agreed. "Apparently everyone took their vitamins today!"

Well, almost everyone.

The only batter who struggled was Marty, who seemed to bounce the ball weakly back to the mound every time—when he made contact at all.

After whiffing on his final three swings, Marty threw his bat down in disgust. "Hitting is overrated," he said, pulling off his batting gloves.

Leaning against the backstop, Connor nudged Cody and silently mouthed: "Watch this."

"What about pitching and fielding?" Connor asked Marty.

"*Totally* overrated," Marty said, rising to the bait. "Base-running too. Who cares how fast you are? It's baseball, not a track meet."

Connor let that statement hang in the air for a moment.

Finally he said, "So if hitting's not important, and pitching's not important, and neither is fielding and base-running, how do you win baseball games?"

Marty shot him a knowing look. Then he placed a bony finger to his temple. "You win them up here, guys," he said. "Brain power. Superior IQ. Or as I like to call it, the Loopus Factor."

At this, all the Orioles within earshot cracked up. Marty grinned and said, "My job here is done," and sauntered away. Cody realized it was the first time he had laughed that hard in weeks. He was amazed at how good it felt.

Why can't the good feelings ever last? he wondered as Coach signaled practice to a close. Then Cody remembered the two girls in art class this morning. When he sat down across from them, they had looked at each other and puffed out their cheeks like, *Check out the chunkster*.

Oh, yeah, he said to himself. *That's why.*

5

When you clicked on weight-loss ads, as Cody had done lately, they promised all sorts of fantastic things.

Drop 10 pounds by Friday!
Lose that spare tire by dawn!
Control your appetite with our new
super-secret technique!

Or, he thought, you could do what he was doing now, which was staring at a mound of disgusting-looking steamed crabs and wondering if he'd ever eat anything again. The crabs were piled high in the middle of a picnic table in his neighbors' backyard. Cody had no trouble imagining that he could get sick from just *looking* at these things.

"They're from the Gulf of Mexico," Mr. Hoffman said as he grabbed a big crab dusted with orange seasoning and plopped it on the paper plate in front of him. "Probably from Louisiana. It's too early for our Chesapeake Bay crabs. But we wanted to welcome you folks to the neighborhood, Baltimore-style."

Oh, Cody thought, you shouldn't have. And he meant it. *You really, really shouldn't have.*

Looking around, Cody noticed that he seemed to be the only one not having a good time on this warm Sunday afternoon.

Paul and Joan Hoffman and their daughter, Jessica, who was in a couple of Cody's classes at York Middle, were enthusiastically whacking the crabs with little wooden mallets and digging out the yucky-looking white stuff inside. So were Cody's mom and dad, who, once they'd been given a quick lesson on the art of crab picking, had taken to it like seasoned pros.

Apparently there was a ritual to be followed. First, the Hoffmans explained, you pulled off the little legs and licked off the seasoning. Then you cracked open the claws and dug out the meat. Then you did the same thing with the shell. But when you cracked open the shell, Cody saw, you found some *really* yucky-looking green stuff.

"That's called the mustard," Mr. Hoffman explained. "Some people like it. It's sort of the crab's, um, liver and pancreas."

Oh, yum, yum, Cody thought. The liver and pancreas!

He looked down at the half-open crab in front of him and felt his stomach recoil.

Whatever happened to welcoming your new neighbors with a cookout? he wondered. With, like, hamburgers and hot dogs? Wouldn't that be a nice thing to do? Who didn't like all-American food like that?

Or how about a pizza party? That would be even better! No fuss, no muss for the hosts. Although pizza, Cody had to admit, was probably not the best thing for a thirteen-year-old ballplayer newly determined to lose weight so he wouldn't be the butt of jokes for the entire population of York Middle School, not to mention one particular member of his Babe Ruth League team.

Cody went back to listlessly whacking a crab claw, hoping no one would notice he was too grossed out to eat any of the stuff.

Suddenly he was aware of someone standing behind him.

"Let me guess," Jessica began. "Wisconsin Boy is semi–freaking out about now. He's never even *seen* steamed crabs, never mind eaten them. And the idea of popping a chunk of that white stuff in his mouth is making him want to hurl. Is that pretty much the story so far?"

Cody nodded weakly and felt his face growing red. Jessica was a slim, athletic-looking girl with long blond hair and big blue eyes. Gazing into those eyes now reminded Cody that he never knew what to say in the presence of pretty girls.

He tugged his shirt down over his belly and managed a weak smile. Immediately, alarm bells went off in his head: *No, don't give her the fake smile! The one that makes you look like your grandma just kissed you!*

"If it makes you feel better," Jessica said, plopping down next to him, "I didn't like crabs the first time I tried them, either."

Actually, Cody thought, that does make me feel better.

"Of course," Jessica said, "I was only two years old at the time."

She laughed uproariously and punched him playfully on the shoulder. "Time to man up, Wisconsin Boy," she said. "Here, watch how the pros do it."

Expertly, she cracked a shell in half and dug out a thick slice of meat with her knife. "Okay, try this," she said, holding it out for him. "This is the best part. You'll think you died and went to heaven."

Staring at the glistening white chunk, Cody could imagine dying, but not heaven. Increasingly, it was feeling like the opposite of heaven—that other place with all the flames and wailing and suffering. A wave of nausea came over him.

But everyone at the table was looking at him now, waiting to see what he'd do. If he didn't at least try the stuff, he'd look like the world's biggest wuss. With his luck, it would get around school too: *Know that fat kid who looks like he's pretty much eaten the world's entire food supply? He wouldn't even try a teeny piece of crabmeat! What a loser!*

Before he could change his mind, Cody grabbed the meat and popped it in his mouth. He took a couple of quick bites and swallowed. It took a second or two for his brain to process how it tasted.

Which was . . . *Whoa! Not bad! Not bad at all.*

It didn't taste fishy, as he'd expected. Instead it was sweet and tangy. And the little bit of seasoning on it was enough to make his lips tingle.

Cody waited a moment, milking the drama for all it was worth. Finally he smiled and gave the thumbs-up sign as everyone else at the table chuckled.

Jessica clapped him on the back. "I knew you had it in you!" she said. "Sometimes you need a little faith."

Sounds like one of Mom's country songs, Cody thought. But now he was secretly glad Jessica had embarrassed him into trying the crabs. And for the next hour, he happily whacked away at the creatures with everyone else, devouring the succulent meat with gusto.

This new town is still weird, he thought. But this is one pastime I could definitely get used to.

When they had all eaten their fill and helped clean up, Jessica went into the garage. She returned with a ball and two gloves, tossing one to Cody.

"Let's hope you're better at this than at conversation," she said, laughing and punching him on the shoulder again.

Cody felt his cheeks get warm again. It dawned on him that he had yet to say a word since arriving at the Hoffmans'.

"Sorry," he said. "I'm usually not this quiet."

"Quiet?!" Jessica said. "My greyhound talks more than you do!"

Cody smiled. A comedian, he thought. Just what I need.

They stood twenty yards apart and started playing catch. As soon as he put on the glove, Cody could feel the nervousness leaving him, replaced by the calm that baseball always delivered. Right away Cody was impressed with Jessica. She threw with an easy, fluid motion, snapping her wrist and following through perfectly, the ball popping into his glove with a loud *THWACK!*

"Wow!" Cody said after her first couple of throws.

Jessica nodded. "I know, I know," she said. "I don't throw like a girl, right?"

"Not like any girl I know," Cody said. "And better than most guys."

"That's 'cause I've played rec-league softball since I was five," Jessica said. "I'd rather be playing baseball. But they won't let me. Guess they're afraid I'll show up the boys."

She grinned and blew a stray hair from her face. Then she fired another missile to Cody, who was already backing up a few steps.

"So, what do you think of your new school?" Jessica asked.

Oh, let's see, Cody thought. I don't have any friends. I get teased constantly about my weight. I sit with all the losers at lunch. Other than that, everything's just fine.

But all he said to Jessica was, "It's okay, I guess."

"Hey, there's a ringing endorsement!" Jessica said, firing another heater at him. "Maybe that could be our new motto: *York Middle: We're Just Okay!*"

This time Cody had to laugh. He liked Jessica already. The girl was funny and smart and, well, not bad-looking, either. And she could throw a baseball through a brick wall! How could you not like someone like that?

"It's really a great school, Wisconsin Boy," she continued. "You'll see that, once you get used to it."

Cody shrugged.

"I guess," he said. "It's just . . . not everyone seems thrilled to see a new kid."

"Oh?" she said, looking at him quizzically.

But Cody didn't feel like getting into the whole business of exactly who wasn't welcoming him with open arms—especially the big, hairy guy on his baseball team. So he quickly changed the subject.

"Let's have a fly-ball contest," he said. "First to drop one loses."

They played catch for another fifteen minutes until Cody's mom and dad said it was time to go. Then Cody and his family thanked the Hoffmans for a wonderful afternoon and headed home.

Cody couldn't wait to go on Facebook and tell his friends back in Wisconsin how he'd spent the past few hours.

Eating delicious steamed crabs! And playing catch with a pretty girl whose fastball was better than the coach's son's!

Not exactly a bad day for the kid.

It was a perfect evening for the Orioles' season opener against the Angels. The warm rays of the sun hinted at all the long, lazy summer days to come.

Cody checked the lineup card taped to the dugout wall and was happy to see he was batting fifth, a real slugger's spot. Willie, with his blinding speed, was leading off, followed by Robby, Jordy, and Connor, with Dante batting sixth.

"Our own Murderers' Row!" Coach exulted, then explained that the nickname was given to the first six batters of the powerful New York Yankees teams of the late 1920s, a lineup that included the great Babe Ruth and Lou Gehrig.

Cody was so excited about playing baseball again that he'd had trouble falling asleep the night before. After pacing restlessly around the house, he had oiled his glove twice, bent the brim of his Orioles cap over and over again until it had achieved the perfect angle, and tried on his new uniform three different times.

Checking himself in the mirror, he was shocked to see how small the uniform was. The jersey was stretched across his belly, revealing every bulge. Plus, he could barely button his pants at the waist, and the pants legs barely reached below his calves. When Coach had handed out uniforms at their last practice, he had taken Cody aside and said he was sorry there wasn't a larger one.

Not as sorry as I am, Cody had said to himself, staring forlornly at his lumpy reflection. No one was going to mistake him for one of those lean, smiling kids who model youth baseball uniforms in the Dick's Sporting Goods commercials. If anything, he looked like he was auditioning for the thirteen-and-under version of *The Biggest Loser*.

If he needed any more incentive to eat sensibly, which he had already been doing lately, the uniform was a good one. And the one-on-one basketball he played with Jessica in her driveway every evening could only help. She was as good at hoops as she was at softball—big surprise.

Cody just wanted the teasing about his weight to stop. If losing a few pounds would give him more of an edge on the field, well, that was an added bonus. In fact, he was so pumped for the Orioles' opener that he had hardly thought about Dante all day in school. Looking around now, he spotted him loosening his arm with Yancy, the two of them laughing about something.

Dante laughing—maybe that was a good sign, Cody thought. Maybe Dante had finally accepted the fact that he wasn't playing third base and he was now totally cool with left field. Maybe the big guy was through messing with him. Maybe he'd even turn out to be a great teammate, cheering and encouraging Cody no matter what position he played or how well or poorly he performed.

Yeah, right. But a guy could always hope.

The new Murderers' Row didn't take long to show off its power, as the Orioles took a 4–0 lead over the Angels in the first inning.

Willie led off with a walk and stole second before the Angels catcher even got the ball out of his mitt. Robbie flied out to center field—too shallow for Willie to advance. But Jordy drove him home with a double in the gap in left-center and Connor delivered an RBI double of his own down the right-field line to make it 2–0.

In the on-deck circle, Cody quietly gave a last-minute pep talk to his bat. As he walked to the plate, he heard snickering from the Angels dugout. And the pitcher, a kid he recognized from lunch period, was smirking and exchanging glances with the third baseman, the two making it clear they were seeing something really funny at the plate right now.

Cody dug into the batter's box and took a couple of practice swings. The message behind the pitcher's smile was clear: *What's this fat boy going to do with that fancy bat? He looks like he can barely make it to first base, never mind get a hit.* Cody could feel his anger rise. He gripped the bat tightly and waved it in tiny circles, trying to look menacing, the way Prince Fielder did right before he blasted the cover off the ball.

How great would it be to knock that arrogant smile off the pitcher's face? Cody thought. But this wasn't a Hollywood movie. The kid wasn't going to serve up a batting-practice fastball just to make Cody feel better. He'd have to work for every hit he got, just like always.

The first two pitches were low and in the dirt. Cody checked his swing on both. Now the kid threw a big, looping curveball that seemed to break from somewhere around the parking lot. It missed the plate by a foot.

Cody stepped out and took a deep breath. A 3 and 0 count. No way the pitcher wanted to walk him. *Give the fat kid a free pass? Please.* The rest of the Angels would never let him hear the end of it! No, this next pitch would be right down Main Street, the middle of the plate.

And when it arrived . . .

Careful, don't be too eager, Cody reminded himself. Don't lunge at it. Short, compact swing. Just hit the ball somewhere, like Dad always says. And hit it hard. Which is exactly what he did. The next pitch was a belt-high fastball, so tantalizing, Cody could feel his eyes bugging out of his head. But somehow he kept his hands back until the last second and uncoiled from his hips with a quick, level swing, his shoulders, arms, and hands following in a perfect symphony.

It was one of those swings, ball meeting bat on the sweet spot of the barrel, that feels effortless. Cody knew it was gone the moment he hit it. He paused to watch anyway as the ball soared over the left-field fence, and the Orioles' dugout exploded with noise and chants of "CO-DY! CO-DY!"

Running to first with a big smile on his face, he thought: Maybe this wasn't a Hollywood movie, with a slow-motion sequence of his home run swing and rousing music as he circled the bases. But it felt like the next best thing.

As he rounded third, Cody was struck by a sudden impulse. He waited until Coach high-fived him and turned his head. Then he reached out quickly and smacked the third baseman on his butt as he ran by.

"Fat power, bay-bee!" he said in a low voice.

The third baseman scowled and looked down at the ground. The pitcher wasn't looking at him, either, Cody noticed, having developed a sudden fascination for the laces in the webbing of his glove.

The Orioles' dugout had emptied now, and his teammates were gathered around home plate. As he jumped on the plate, he was engulfed in a knot of whooping players pounding him on the back and smacking him on the helmet.

But there was one conspicuous absence from this happy throng, Cody noticed. Dante remained in the on-deck circle, leaning on his bat and looking off into the distance, ignoring the impromptu celebration.

The rest of the game seemed to fly by as Robbie threw a three-hitter and the Orioles continued to pound all three Angels pitchers who took the mound. Even Dante got in on the action, driving in a run in the fifth inning with a sharp single up the middle. Nobody cheered harder for Dante than Cody—he practically flew out of the dugout to let the big guy know how happy he was about his RBI. Maybe *that* would get him on Dante's good side.

The final score was Orioles 9, Angels 2. As the two teams lined up to slap hands, Cody was relieved not to hear any snickering. The Angels pitcher, in fact, actually mumbled, "Good hitting." And the Angels coach made it a point to stop and shake his hand and say, "You got a real quick bat there, son."

Looking up in the stands, Cody saw his mom waving and giving the thumbs-up sign.

"Great game, boys!" she shouted. Then she blew a kiss at Cody and said, "Meet you at the car."

But Cody was in no hurry to leave. This was too much fun. He took his time changing out of his spikes and gathering up his bat and glove and packing his equipment bag. Then he walked up to the parking lot with Jordy and Connor, the three of them talking excitedly about their first win until the two boys ran off to catch their rides.

It was almost dark now. Up ahead, Cody saw the taillights of his mom's car, parked off to one side. She'd be sitting inside with the dome light on, reading a book or doing a crossword puzzle, the way she always did when she had a few minutes to spare.

He took off his cap and broke into a trot. The cool evening breeze felt good as it rippled through his hair.

Suddenly he felt a push from behind and he found himself tumbling headfirst into the gravel. Out of the corner of his eye, he saw a shadowy figure run off between two cars.

"I warned you, fat boy!" a voice hissed. "And you didn't listen."

Cody found his dad's office disappointing. Steve Parker was assigned to the Northern District detective unit and worked in a low-slung, modern building off a busy highway. To Cody, it looked pretty much like his dad's old office back in Milwaukee: row after row of drab cubicles, each with a chair and computer, case files stacked on top of desks, phone books and notepads tossed everywhere, and a coffeepot off to one side.

It reminded him of the insurance agency where his uncle Tim worked in Connecticut. Weren't police stations supposed to be exciting places? Places where tough-looking men and no-nonsense women shouted into phones and interrogated bad guys and gulped down steaming coffee from Styrofoam cups before jumping into their cars and dashing off with lights flashing to another crime scene? Or was that just on TV and in the movies?

When his dad had picked him up from practice and said he needed to swing by the office to get his mail, Cody had been excited to see the place. But the only thing even remotely exciting about it, he thought, was the bright red

M&M's dispenser in the corner that someone had brought in, probably to amuse any young kids who visited and got bored. Which wouldn't take long, judging by the look of things.

"Seems there's been some trouble at your school," his dad said, sitting at his desk and studying his laptop. "Couple of instances of petty theft at York Middle. County cops are handling it."

Cody nodded distractedly. He was getting hungry and hoped his dad would hurry up so they could get home to eat.

"You're awfully quiet tonight," his dad said. "Everything okay?"

Cody looked out the window at the rush hour traffic snaking up Cold Spring Lane, a sea of white-yellow headlights and red brake lights as far as he could see. How to explain the charming Dante Rizzo, who seemed like the angriest kid he'd ever come across? And did he even want to get into this with his dad, who was already feeling guilty about moving his family to Baltimore and worried that his son was having a tough time adjusting?

"Everything's fine," Cody said. "I'm a little tired, that's all."

His dad grunted and went back to his mail.

The night before in the parking lot, after Cody had stumbled to his mom's car with scrapes on his face and hands, he told her that he'd tripped over a curb in the darkness.

Seeing the look of alarm on her face, he'd added, "You know how clumsy I am."

But after making sure he wasn't badly hurt, Kate Parker had looked at him skeptically.

"So, you tripped," she'd said, drawing out the words. "Over a curb."

And when Cody had nodded—*sure, that's what happened, honest*—Kate Parker had started the car, given him another sideways glance, and said, "Ohhh-kay. Let's get home and clean you up."

Okay, fine, it was a lame story. Mega-lame. Cody could see that now. What thirteen-year-old kid trips over a curb? Your ninety-year-old great-grandma with bad eyesight and a walker—maybe *she* trips over a curb. Not a young, active kid, no matter how hulking he is. But it was all he could come up with at the time.

Cody picked up a copy of *The Baltimore Sun* and glanced at the sports section. There were a few other detectives in the room, making phone calls, looking through files, and tapping away on their computers. A police scanner squawked unintelligibly in one corner.

After a minute or two, Cody put down the newspaper and took a deep breath.

"Dad," he said, "were there any bullies in your school when you were a kid?"

His dad swiveled around in his chair and peered at him over his reading glasses.

"Someone bothering you?" he asked.

"No, no," Cody said, trying to keep his voice light. "Just curious."

Steve Parker leaned back and clasped his hands behind his head and nodded. "Max Wheeler was the big bully in eighth grade," he said. "We called him Mad Max. Everyone was terrified of him. But, for some reason, he took a particular dislike to me."

"Why you?"

"I was never exactly sure. I got pretty good grades. And I was a decent ballplayer. Maybe he resented that. Plus, I think he thought I was a rich kid. Which I definitely wasn't. Anyway, he made my life hell, that's for sure."

"What did he do?" Cody asked, sitting up now.

"Oh, the usual stuff, right out of Bullying 101. He pushed me into lockers. Tripped me a couple of times in the halls. Elbowed me in the chest in gym class once. And he'd wait for me after school too. Just to tell me he was going to kick my butt. Like I hadn't already gotten the message."

Steve Parker shook his head at the memory and smiled softly, letting his gaze drift out the window. "He was a big, strong kid, Max was," he continued. "Way bigger than me. My heart would start pounding whenever I saw him."

Cody nodded. *Yeah, know the feeling.*

On the other hand, he couldn't imagine his dad being afraid of anyone or anything now. A few years ago, when the whole family was on a white-water rafting trip in Wisconsin, his dad had leaped into the churning Menominee River to rescue a little kid who had fallen overboard.

And just last year Steve Parker had made the six o'clock news for foiling an early morning holdup. He had stopped in a convenience store for coffee when a knucklehead with a knife attempted to scoop the contents of the cash register and flee. Cody's dad chased the robber for two blocks, drew his weapon, and forced the guy to surrender as pedestrians scattered for cover.

The *Milwaukee Journal Sentinel* ran the story with a photo of Detective Parker being thanked by the store owner. For days after, their phone rang with friends and neighbors and relatives calling to congratulate the hero.

Not that Cody's dad would ever stand for anyone calling him a hero.

"I was just doing my job," he told everyone. But Cody had never felt prouder of his dad. It was one of the reasons he wanted to be a police officer himself someday, although when he had confessed this to his mother, she had turned pale and said, "Please, sweetie. You're going to make your mom old before her time."

"So how'd you get Mad Max to leave you alone?" Cody asked.

His dad chuckled and turned back from the window. "Little bit of ingenuity—and a whole lot of luck," he said. "One day, I had just *had* it with Max. I was tired of being bullied. Tired of being afraid all the time. So I decided to stand up to him. Sure, I knew I'd get my butt kicked. But maybe then he'd leave me alone.

"So the big showdown was going to be that day, right after school. And I figured I was a dead man. But that afternoon, I noticed something in science class. We were studying reptiles. All of a sudden, we heard this loud gasp. Everyone turned around. It was Max. He was staring at a picture of a snake that was being passed around. And he was white as a ghost!

"Well," Cody's dad continued, dropping his voice for dramatic effect, "guess what I had in my terrarium at home?"

Cody grinned and rubbed his hands together. This was going to be good.

"So I put off the big showdown for a day. And the next morning I bring Herbie, my pet garter snake, to school. Which wasn't exactly easy. See, we didn't carry backpacks back then. I brought him in a brown paper bag. Everyone thought it was my lunch."

Cody tried to imagine what would happen at York Middle if a kid sat down in the cafeteria and pulled a two-foot garter snake out of his lunch bag. They'd probably evacuate the school and bring in a SWAT team.

"Now, school lets out and I start walking home," his dad continued. "And there's ol' Mad Max, waiting for me on the corner. I'm swinging the lunch bag like there's nothing in there but a peanut-butter-and-jelly sandwich I didn't eat, or a cookie or something. Poor Herbie probably thought he was on a carnival ride.

"Naturally, Max blocks my path. Then he pushes me in the chest and says, 'Let's play a game, Parker. You give me what's in the bag, and I won't smash your face.' 'Okay,' I say. 'But can this little guy play too?' Then I pull out Herbie."

Cody whooped. Then, remembering where he was, he looked around sheepishly.

"You should've seen Max's face," his dad went on. "His eyes almost bugged out of his head! He actually started trembling. I almost felt sorry for him. Then he turned and ran away as fast as he could. And he never bothered me again."

Cody and his dad sat in silence for a moment. Steve Parker couldn't stop smiling at the memory. Cody couldn't stop grinning and shaking his head in wonder. It was one of the finest stories he had ever heard.

"Anyway," his dad said, "if you ever need help with someone like Mad Max, you know where to turn."

Cody nodded and his dad stood and slung his laptop bag over his shoulder. "All right, let's get home for dinner," he said. "Your mother will be wondering where we are."

But by the time they had said good-bye to the other detectives and were heading toward his dad's car, Cody was back to thinking glumly about his predicament.

For an instant he wondered if Dante was scared of snakes.

Nah, he decided.

More likely, it was the other way around.

"The boy's the size of a refrigerator," Willie said, watching wide-eyed as the kid at the plate launched a moon shot over the outfield fence.

"No, he's bigger than that," Connor said in a hushed voice. "He's the size of a sequoia."

"Even his muscles have muscles," Jordy said.

It was ten days later and the 5–0 Orioles were getting set to take on the 5–0 Yankees in their biggest test to date. The Orioles were supposed to be warming up now, stretching and loosening their arms down the right-field line. Except everyone kept stealing glances at Justin Mallory, the Yankees' big first baseman, as he pounded one pitch after another in batting practice.

"Is that a tattoo on his right arm?" Marty asked. "Or just a shadow from his massive biceps flexing?"

"My guess is massive biceps flexing," Jordy said.

Robbie, the Orioles' starting pitcher, was actually starting to flinch at the ungodly sound Justin's bat made—*WHAM!*—each time it met a ball.

"If he hits a line drive back to the mound," Robbie said,

"it might literally go through my chest."

"What's the worst that could happen?" Willie said. "It severs your lungs and your heart pops out. Big deal."

The rest of the Orioles chuckled and went back to their warm-ups. Actually, even seeing this awesome display of power from Justin, they were feeling pretty confident about themselves. After all, they were on a nice roll, having crushed the Tigers 9–1 in their last game, and beaten the Red Sox 6–2 before that.

Cody was feeling more relaxed with his new team. He had gotten off to a great start at the plate and was playing well at third base too. And it didn't hurt that his sprawling catch of a line drive with the bases loaded in the bottom of the sixth inning had been the game-saving play against the Red Sox. He wished Jessica had been there to see it.

There was another reason his stress level was down. Dante had missed the last two games and hadn't been seen in school, either. Rumor was that he'd been sick in bed.

And people talk about the flu like it's a *bad* thing, Cody thought, smiling at his little joke.

Now that Dante was back, Cody should have been nervous again, but he was actually glad to see him because it meant the Orioles were again at full strength. They would need to be in order to beat the Yankees, who were supposed to have excellent pitching to go along with the human rocket launcher that was Justin Mallory.

"Bring it in," Coach said, summoning them to the dugout.

As the Orioles gathered around him, he read the lineup card. Then he looked up, studied his team for a moment, and grinned.

"I saw you guys checking out Justin," he said. "Don't let him psych you out. He puts his pants on one leg at a time just like you do. He's human, boys. I can assure you of that."

"Yeah, right," Marty whispered. "I don't think you could *get* pants over those tree-trunk legs!"

"He's human the way The Hulk's human," Willie muttered.

A few minutes later the Orioles took the field, and they found themselves in trouble almost immediately. The problem was obvious: Robbie was way too amped up. For whatever reason—Cody figured it had something to do with Robbie's fear of giving up a tape-measure homer to Justin—he was rearing back and overthrowing to the Yankees batters.

He walked the first two on eight straight balls, earning a visit to the mound from Joey Zinno. When Robbie walked the third batter on a 3–1 count to load the bases, Coach called time and popped out of the dugout to settle down his pitcher. This time, Cody, Connor, Willie, and Jordy jogged over to listen.

"Robbie, take a deep breath," Coach said.

Robbie nodded and gulped several times.

"I said take a deep breath, not swallow all the air in the universe," Coach said.

Robbie nodded again. His face was pale.

"I should probably just relax," he said.

"That would be a splendid idea," Coach said.

"And throw strikes," Robbie said.

"Strikes are always good," Coach said.

"If they hit it, they hit it," Robbie continued. "That's why I have seven guys behind me, right?"

"Right," Coach said.

"Just aim for Joey's glove," Robbie said. "Pitch and catch. Everything else will take care of itself, right?"

His dad nodded. "You're stealing all my lines. But I'm glad we had this little chat."

As Coach turned to leave, the Orioles infielders looked at each other and grinned. Robbie had heard his dad's pitching advice so often he could recite it in his sleep. He picked up the ball and slammed it into his glove with a look of renewed determination.

"I'm okay now," he said. Then he grew pale again when he spotted Justin in the on-deck circle, lazily swinging a couple of huge bats over his head as if they were toothpicks.

"Remember, he's human," Connor said, smacking Robbie on the butt.

"Puts his pants on one leg at a time," Willie said.

Cody grinned, then quickly put his glove in front of his face so Coach couldn't see. The smack talk that ballplayers laid on each other was just as bad in Baltimore as it was in Milwaukee.

Somehow, though, Robbie managed to settle down. Now he wasn't trying to blow the ball past Justin. Instead, he threw two changeups for strikes that fooled the Yankees' cleanup hitter, and followed them with two high fastballs, hoping the big guy would swing at a bad pitch.

No such luck. The count was 2–2. Justin frowned and stepped out of the box and took a couple of vicious practice swings. Robbie paced around the mound, rubbing the ball and thinking about what to throw.

Please, not a fastball, Cody said to himself. *It'll end up in the Inner Harbor.*

"Now you're pitching!" Coach shouted to his son, pointing to his own temple. "Use your head!"

And Robbie did just that. With Justin practically twitching at the plate and salivating for a fastball, Robbie threw him a slow curve. It was a great pitch. Justin seemed to freeze for an instant before lunging awkwardly at it. The guy was so big he was able, even at the last minute, to stick the bat out far enough for a weak single down the left-field line. Dante hustled over to retrieve it, but not before two runs scored.

Everyone—including Justin, probably—knew it was a lucky hit. But Robbie didn't let it rattle him, striking out the next three batters to end the inning. As the Orioles hustled in, one by one they slapped gloves with Robbie and said, "Nice job."

Yes, they were down, 2–0. But the idea that Robbie had held Justin in the ballpark almost made them want to celebrate.

"Boys, it's our game now," Coach said. "Robbie's back. He's not pitching like a knucklehead anymore."

All eyes shot to Robbie, who bowed dramatically, then pointed at his teammates and said, "That's *Mister* Knucklehead to you guys."

The rest of the Orioles cracked up. Even Dante was laughing. Cody shook his head in wonder. At times, he thought, playing for this team was like stepping into a real, live sitcom.

"Now that we're all on the same page," Coach continued, grinning at Robbie, "let's get some hits."

But that proved to be easier said than done. For the first time this season, the Orioles' bats were struggling. A single by Dante in the third inning and back-to-back walks to Willie and Robbie in the fifth accounted for their only base runners. Cody flied out to left field twice and hit a bouncer back to the pitcher his third time up, despite silently pleading with his bat each time he walked to the plate.

"What's going on here?" Coach said. "Murderers' Row is more like Murmurers' Row."

The only good news for the Orioles was that Justin actually *did* seem to be human after all, going 0 for 2 after his excuse-me swing that drove in the two Yankees runs. The Yankees were still clinging to their 2–0 lead when the Orioles came up in the bottom of the sixth inning. The Orioles were down to their last three outs. If they didn't get something going right away, they'd pick up their first loss of the season.

"All right, everyone in here," Coach said as he gathered the Orioles around him. "Look," he continued, scanning each player's face, "I believe in you guys. And I really think we're going to win. But just to make sure, Cody's going to lead us in the team prayer."

Now all eyes were on Cody—who went into an immediate flop-sweat panic.

His mind raced: *We have a team prayer? No one told me about a team prayer, did they? Or was I not paying attention? Because I don't remember any—*

Just then, the rest of the Orioles burst out laughing.

"Relax," Coach said, grinning. "We don't have a team prayer. Or if we do, it goes like this: *Please let us hit it where they ain't.* That's the oldest prayer in baseball. Now, let's win this game!"

Cody was so relieved, he nearly slumped against the railing as the rest of the team—except Dante, who was back in full glower mode—pounded him on the back and shouted, "Gotcha!" Then they put their hands in the middle of a circle and shouted, "One, two, three . . . Orioles!"

Now Cody found himself smiling. Boy, he thought, Coach sure does have a strange sense of humor. But he had to admit it was a great joke, even if the joke was on him.

Just as Coach had intended, the joke seemed to loosen up the Orioles—and give them new life.

Willie led off with a double against the new Yankees pitcher, a hard-throwing lefty. After Robbie lifted a lazy fly ball to the third baseman for the first out, Jordy followed with an RBI single up the middle to pull the Orioles to within one. Connor followed him with a single to put runners on first and third.

The Orioles were alive and kicking.

As Cody tapped the doughnut off his bat in the on-deck circle and headed for the plate, the noise from the stands was deafening. The Orioles were up and cheering in their dugout too, with Marty banging two bats together, making them sound like the thundersticks fans banged at pro basketball games.

Knowing Marty, Cody thought, I wouldn't be surprised if he brings *vuvuzelas* to our next game.

Now it was the Yankees' pitcher who was caught up in the moment and overthrowing. His first two pitches were high and would have sailed all the way to the backstop if not for two great plays by the catcher. But with the count 2–0, he grooved a fastball over the plate, and Cody turned on it. It wasn't the best hit he ever had, but it was a sharp single to left field to score Jordy.

Then the Orioles caught a huge break. Charging the ball to keep Connor from advancing, the Yankees left fielder overran it. It rolled ten feet past him, and by the time he hustled to retrieve it, Connor was steaming across the plate with the winning run.

Final score: 3–2 Orioles. They were still undefeated. As the Orioles poured out of their dugout to celebrate and Cody ran in to join them, he glimpsed something out of the corner of his eye.

Not everyone, it seemed, had raced out of the O's dugout. Sitting there, with his cap pulled low over his eyes and his arms crossed, was Dante. And, once again, he didn't seem too happy.

But Cody had no time to think about that as the Orioles whooped and jumped on him and pounded him on the back. Then the two teams lined up to slap hands. When Cody spotted the sad-looking kid who had made the costly error in left, he said quietly, "Nice try," and the kid nodded in appreciation.

Looking around moments later, Cody noticed Dante was already gone. He was glad to see his mom was still in the stands, though. He decided he'd walk to the parking lot with her, just in case Dante was planning another surprise face-in-the-gravel chat.

Somehow, Cody doubted that would happen. But he had a feeling he'd be hearing from the big guy soon enough.

And he didn't think Dante would be saying "Nice game."

"Get ready for a beat down, fat boy!" were the exact words out of Dante's mouth the next time they met.

This was at 7:30 the next morning, right after Cody stepped off the school bus at York Middle. There might have been more to his cheery greeting, but it was hard to tell because the thug had him in a headlock now and was dragging him around in a circle and squeezing his ears, like WWE wrestlers do before they ram their opponent's head into the turnbuckle.

"I'm sick of your big ugly mug!" Dante snarled, digging his elbows into Cody's face. "Time to rearrange it!"

It had all happened so fast. One minute Cody was making his way to the school's side entrance with all the other kids; the next minute someone grabbed him from behind.

For an instant, Cody got a whiff of incredibly bad breath—had the guy eaten sardines and pepperoni for breakfast?—before Dante spun him around and got him in the headlock.

By now a crowd of students had gathered to watch, apparently assuming a butt-whipping would be more interesting than, say, first-period Algebra or English.

"Isn't it a little early for this?" Cody managed to gasp before Dante tightened his grip even more.

Cody knew that none of the kids forming a circle around them would be jumping in to help him. No, he was still the new kid after all these weeks.

Oh, sure, his social status at York Middle had improved slightly in the last month. For one thing, he had finally graduated from the nerd/misfit table at lunch and now sat with Willie and Connor and Jordy, who were considered three of the coolest kids in eighth grade. But none of his new buddies was around now. And Cody knew he still wasn't exactly Mr. Popular with the rest of the student body.

Besides, even if someone was brave enough—or foolish enough—to intervene, that would be only the beginning of the kid's problems. Because not only would he have to deal with Dante, he'd also eventually have to deal with the infamous Rottweiler Twins.

As Dante snarled and squeezed and whirled him around, Cody quickly considered his options. They seemed limited at best.

He could hope one of the teachers on bus duty would spot the knot of whooping kids and come over and break it up. But with all the buses already here—Cody's was usually the last to arrive—most of the teachers had already gone inside to their homerooms.

Or he could hope the sky would crack open and a large lightning bolt would land at Dante's feet, creating an enormous fissure in the ground that would swallow him. The way it was looking now, the odds of that happening were actually better than the odds of a teacher saving him.

"How's the air down there, fat boy?" Dante was saying now. "Getting hard to breathe?"

It sure was. Whatever you do, Cody told himself, don't let them see you cry. That would be disastrous. By lunch-time it would be all over the school. *Did you see that fat kid blubbering when Dante whupped him this morning? The little baby couldn't stop crying!* Oh, that would be all he needed.

But the tears *were* coming—he could feel it. His face was hot and sweaty, and he thought his head was going to pop like a grape any minute. Not to mention that he was getting really dizzy from all this whirling around. Now it felt like he was going to hurl too.

Great. He'd be a crying, puking mess—what a nice image that would be.

"Can we . . . talk?" Cody croaked. But Dante just squeezed harder. Apparently that was his way of saying no.

Suddenly, the grip around Cody's head loosened. He heard the big guy cry out, "Owww! Hey, that hurt!"

And now another voice cut through the din, a familiar voice shouting, "Let him go, you big goon! Or I'll kick you again!"

Shaking free of Dante, Cody looked up, rubbing his eyes. It was Jessica. She was in a karate stance now, her right leg coiled to deliver another looping blow. She wore a red sweatshirt with the hood up, strands of blond hair cascading down each shoulder.

Between his dizziness and his blurred vision, Cody wondered for an instant if he was dreaming. Or maybe Jessica really *was* some kind of secret modern-day superhero. Mild-mannered, crab-picking eighth grader one moment, avenging crusader for truth and justice the next.

She was definitely in the avenging mode now. Her eyes were narrow slits, her face an angry mask. Cody couldn't believe it was the same happy-go-lucky girl he had shot hoops with the day before.

"Guess we should all be getting along to class," Jessica said evenly.

Dante seemed as stunned to see this blond, hooded vigilante as Cody was. He stared at her slack-jawed, rubbing his sore arm as he considered his next move. But Cody could see something else in his expression now too.

Was it fear? Humiliation? Or a combination of the two? Cody wasn't sure, but he had seen that look on his face once before—on that first day of practice, after Dante had missed the first two ground balls Coach had hit his way.

For several seconds, Dante said nothing. Then his shoulders sagged, and he picked his backpack off the ground.

"Okay, okay," he muttered, shoving Cody aside. "We'll pick this up later, fat boy."

Dante began pushing his way through the knot of kids. Then he turned, shot one last look at Cody, and sneered. "You won't always have a girl around to protect you."

As the rest of the kids wandered off to class—did they seem disappointed not to see someone get pounded?—Cody slumped against the wall to catch his breath.

He wasn't sure what bothered him most now: how scared he'd been of Dante, or how relieved he'd been when Jessica came to his aid like some pint-sized Wonder Woman.

Where did she learn all that karate stuff? As he was being smothered in a headlock, he hadn't seen the kick she'd landed on Dante. It must have been a beauty. The guy would probably be rubbing his bruise all day.

Just then, Jessica walked over and smiled and put an arm on his shoulder.

"Wisconsin Boy," she said softly, "what in the world have you gotten yourself into?"

Cody watched Prince Fielder saunter from the Milwaukee Brewers' dugout to the on-deck circle, holding his thick bat by the barrel and gazing around nonchalantly. At the plate, the Brewers' Ryan Braun was digging in against Baltimore Orioles right-hander Jeremy Guthrie. But Cody couldn't take his eyes off his idol, the Prince of Power himself.

It was two days later, a warm Sunday afternoon, and Cody was watching his first game at Camden Yards, the downtown home of the Orioles. His dad called it "the Taj Mahal of ballparks." By Googling it Cody discovered that the Taj Mahal was a famous building in India. After reading that it was considered one of the most beautiful structures in the world, Cody understood what his dad meant.

Yes, Camden Yards was eye-popping. The grass was a deep, shimmering green—the greenest grass he'd ever seen—mowed in long, perfect diagonal rows. The reddish infield dirt looked as smooth as the felt on a pool table. Cody couldn't imagine a ground ball ever taking a bad hop. And the imposing B&O Warehouse, with its brick facade, loomed behind the right-field stands. If you were a lefty slugger standing in the batter's box, he thought, it must look close enough to touch.

Cody had been to Miller Park in Milwaukee to see the Brewers play lots of times—it was only forty minutes from his old house. But Camden Yards was even nicer. That the Orioles were playing the Brewers in a rare interleague matchup made the day even more special.

"Sorry I couldn't get better seats," Steve Parker said, grinning.

"Yeah, you gotta work on that," Cody said, sipping his lemonade.

"Is this really the best you could do, Steve?" his mom added.

The seats had been a running joke between the three of them all afternoon. Because the fact was, they were sitting in section 36, right behind home plate, courtesy of one of his dad's fellow detectives, who had season tickets and knew Cody was a big Brewers fan.

Cody had never been this close to Prince Fielder before. What he loved about Prince more than anything was how he carried himself: at 260 pounds, he seemed totally at ease with his weight. On JockBio.com, Cody had read that as a kid, Fielder had even appeared in a McDonald's triple cheeseburger commercial with his father, Cecil.

But Cody's favorite story about Prince was this: When he played for the minor-league Nashville Sounds, the guy had to wear number 66. The jerseys were assigned according to size, and he couldn't fit into anything smaller. The only bigger uniform the Sounds handed out that year was to their mascot, Ozzie the tiger, who wore number 68.

Watching Prince take lazy practice swings at the plate now, the bat ending up high over his right shoulder on his perfect follow-through, Cody found himself smiling. His favorite poster of Prince—the one that dominated one wall of his basement—featured the Brewers slugger in an almost identical pose after blasting another mammoth home run. Thinking of his basement made Cody realize he was growing a little less homesick for Milwaukee each day. He was getting used to his new house, with its cozy backyard and big basement, the basement he had basically turned into his own baseball shrine, complete with photos of all the teams he'd been on and posters of his favorite major leaguers. He had even set up an indoor batting cage down there—well, for Wiffle Ball, anyway—complete with netting and a pitcher's mound made of old couch cushions.

If only things were better at school, Cody thought. Especially with one particular classmate . . .

Thinking of Dante, Cody felt the familiar hollow pit in his stomach. Now it looked as if Dante would *never* leave him alone—unless Cody hired Jessica as his full-time bodyguard. Sure, that would look good. Already the other kids were mocking him for letting a girl come to his rescue. Still, he was totally in awe of Jessica's courage. The way she had confronted Dante and refused to back down, even when he gave her that creepy Dante stare—Cody had never seen anything like it. Not outside of a Hollywood movie, anyway.

On the bus ride home from school that day, Jessica had

explained that she had taken karate lessons since she was four years old. She loved it, she said, almost as much as baseball and softball. She was close to getting her black belt.

"My dad says I kick like a mule," she had told Cody.

Remind me never to tick off this girl, Cody thought. Better not foul her too hard in hoops.

Yeah, good ol' Jessica had definitely saved him from a beat down. That fact made it even harder for him to tell his parents about what was going on between him and Dante. Admit he was scared and a girl came to his rescue? Oh, no. Way, way too embarrassing.

Just then they heard a loud *CRACK!* and a roar went up from the crowd. Cody looked up just in time to see Prince drop his bat and admire his latest titanic blast, the ball soaring in the direction of the warehouse and landing out by the concession stands.

"All right, Prince!" Cody yelled, jumping from his seat and drawing annoyed looks from the Orioles fans around him.

Well, excuse me, Cody thought, sitting back down. Didn't realize it was against the law to cheer for your team.

The rest of the game was exciting, with the Orioles eventually pulling out a 2–1 win thanks to home runs by Luke Scott and Adam Jones. But the minute it was over, Cody found himself worrying about Dante again. He was still brooding when he and his parents stopped at a restaurant across the street from the stadium.

Cody ordered a cheeseburger and told the waiter to hold the fries, even though they were about his favorite food in the whole world. But when the burger arrived, Cody took two bites and pushed his plate away, announcing he wasn't very hungry after all.

Steve Parker put down his fork and studied his son.

"Okay," he said quietly. "Tell us about Dante jumping you the other day."

Cody's eyes widened.

He was *so* busted.

Cody was tongue-tied and brain-locked all at once.

"But how did you . . . ?" he finally blurted.

"Mr. Hoffman told us," Steve Parker said. "Jessica came home from school with a bruised foot. She said it was from a karate kick. Her dad made her tell him what happened."

Cody stared down at his plate. Now he had *really* lost his appetite—possibly forever. His dizzying ride on Dante's Headlock Tilt-A-Whirl was about the last thing he wanted to discuss with his parents. But, judging by the expressions on their faces, there would be no changing the subject.

So Cody ran through the whole embarrassing story, starting with the competition at third base, Dante's threats, and the evening he sent Cody on his swan dive through the gravel. Then Cody told them about this latest run-in with York Middle's Bully of the Year candidate and Jessica's heroic intervention, like she was some kind of new Karate Kid.

When he was through, his mom and dad looked at each other and shook their heads softly.

"Maybe in ten years or so, when she gets out of college, we can get Jessica to join the police force," his dad said. "Sounds like a pretty brave girl."

Cody nodded morosely. He poked idly at his burger and said quietly, "Way braver than I was."

His mom patted his arm and said, "Tell us about this Dante."

"For starters he's big and mean, with long, stringy black hair," Cody said. "Sort of like a young Professor Snape. You know, in the Harry Potter movies? Only uglier."

"Yikes."

"He's older too. He looks like he shaves."

"That would explain a few things," his mom said.

"And he always looks ticked off. Like instead of saying hi, he wants to knee you in the groin."

"Sounds like a charmer," his mom said.

"He's got two older brothers too," Cody said. "Vincent and Nick."

"Bet they have the same sweet personality."

"The kids call them the Rottweiler Twins," Cody said.

His mom nodded and said, "Because they're so cute and fuzzy."

"Mess with Dante," Cody went on, "and they mess with you—only twenty times worse. That's what all the kids say."

"Great," his mom said. She sipped her iced tea. "A nasty teenager with muscle behind him. Maybe your dad should get a jail cell ready right now."

Steve Parker nodded, but remained quiet.

"But it's funny," Cody continued. "I've seen this look on

his face. Like he's scared, only he doesn't want anyone to know."

"Maybe he *is* scared," Kate Parker said. "Everyone's scared of something."

The waitress arrived and began clearing the dishes. When she had finished and gone off to get the check, Cody's dad leaned forward and clasped his hands together in front of him. He furrowed his brow and cleared his throat.

Cody recognized the body language right away: his dad was in full problem-solving mode. This is what policemen do; they take action. If a bad guy commits a crime, they think: How do we arrest him and throw him in jail? If an injustice has been committed, their first reaction is, how do we fix it?

"Okay," he said quietly, "now it's time to get Dante to leave you alone. And *you* have to be the one to do it. Agreed?"

Cody nodded. "That's the part that's scary," he said.

"Yep, I remember the feeling," his dad said. "If we called your principal or your teachers, it could get worse, not better. We need to try something else first. We just need a plan. . . ."

He stirred his coffee, seemingly lost in thought, and went on. "He's bigger than you. And stronger too. So a physical confrontation might not be, um, wise. . . ."

"Not unless you want to see me in the emergency room," Cody said mournfully.

"Jessica probably scared him 'cause she knew martial arts—or *looked* like she knew them, anyway," his dad said. "But you say he's seemed scared at other times. . . .Maybe we can work with that. The key is to find something that unsettles him. Like snakes did with Max Wheeler..."

"I have a feeling Dante eats snakes for breakfast," Cody said. "Maybe for lunch and dinner too."

"Unless we try something *really* radical..." his dad said suddenly.

He pulled a ballpoint pen from his shirt pocket and scribbled a couple of sentences on a napkin. Then he pushed the napkin in front of Cody.

Cody couldn't believe what it said, so he read it twice. Then he passed it to his mom, who scanned it and burst out laughing.

"*That's* the big plan?!" Cody said. "*That'll* get Dante to leave me alone?!"

"I've seen it work before," his dad said, grinning. "Sometimes you have to think outside the box."

"OUTSIDE THE BOX?!" Cody almost shouted. "Dad, that's outside the planet! No, that's outside the entire universe!"

Then again, what did he have to lose? If he continued to let Dante torture him, he'd end up like one of those nerdy kids who went through life cringing and trying to disappear before someone said something mean to them or tripped them in the hallway or pushed them into a locker.

He stared down at the napkin again. It was the wackiest plan he had ever heard of.

"Okay," he said. "But if this doesn't work, it was nice knowing you both."

Cody was surprised to be in a good mood
when he arrived at Eddie Murray Field the next day for
the game against the Tigers. For openers, he had gotten a
98 on his social studies test, with his teacher announcing
that it was the highest mark in the class. Even better, Dante
hadn't popped out of a gym locker or burst from a storage closet to beat on him, which meant Cody hadn't been
forced to try out his so-called plan, which was probably
going to result in his face being rearranged in any case.

As he changed into his spikes, he saw Dante off by himself down the third base line, stretching. When their eyes
met, Dante scowled and quickly looked away. Yep, Cody
thought, the big lug still loves me.

Just then Coach came rushing up to see him, a con-
cerned look on his face.

Uh-oh, Cody thought. This can't be good.

It wasn't.

"I need you to pitch today," Coach said.

"WHAT?!"

"Robbie didn't go to school—he's home with a stomach

virus," Coach said. "Mike Cutko's starting for us. Then I'm bringing you in. Probably in the fourth inning."

"Me?" Cody said. His voice suddenly sounded high and squeaky. "Coach, I haven't pitched since I was—"

"You've got the best arm on the team," Coach said. "Well, you and Connor. And your arm is even more accurate than his. You'll do fine. Just throw hard and aim for Joey's mitt. The rest'll take care of itself."

He gave Cody a clap on the back and went off to fill out the lineup card. Still dazed, Cody got his glove and wandered over to where Jordy, Connor, and Willie were warming up.

"Dude, I hear you're on the mound today," Jordy said.

Bet I know what they're thinking, Cody said to himself. *What's Coach doing letting a chunkster like that pitch? Sure, he might be okay at third base, where you don't have to cover a lot of ground. And all that extra weight helps him pop the ball when he's up at bat. But how do you let the guy pitch?*

Yet all Cody said was: "News sure travels fast around here."

There was an awkward silence. Jordy, Willie, and Connor looked at each other. They seemed to be struggling for something to say.

Finally Willie smacked Cody on the butt and said, "Piece of cake, C. You'll shut these sorry Tigers down."

"Don't get your hopes up," Cody said. "I haven't pitched since I was a little kid."

"It's like riding a bicycle," Jordy said. "You never forget how."

"Had a feeling someone was going to say that," Cody said. "But you guys better be ready behind me. I'm going to need some leather flashing today."

Just then Marty pushed his way through the group and draped an arm around Connor's shoulders.

"Listen to me, big man," he said. "Don't worry about this. You need any pitching advice, you come to me, hear?"

The other Orioles looked at each other and rolled their eyes.

"Uh, Marty?" Willie said. "I say this with all due respect. But have you actually ever pitched? In your entire life?"

Now Marty sighed and draped his other arm around Willie's shoulders.

"Willie, Willie, Willie . . ." he said, shaking his head. "Did Columbus ever sail before he discovered America? Did Henry Ford ever drive before he rolled out the Model T automobile? Did Steve Jobs ever sit down at a computer before he developed Apple?"

Willie furrowed his brow. "I'm pretty sure they all—"

"What I'm trying to say," Marty continued, "is that you don't have to actually pitch to know about pitching, son."

"Did you call me *son*?" Willie said. "Marty, you're thirteen years old!"

"This is getting us nowhere," Marty said. Turning back to Cody, he said, "I'm here for you, big man. Think of me as your personal pitching guru."

Despite how nervous he was becoming, Cody found himself grinning. There was something about Marty you had to like. The cluelessness, the over-the-top confidence, the posing as the ultimate authority on any subject . . .

Cody had never seen anything like it. Marty could sure talk a good game, even if he couldn't play one.

The Orioles jumped out to a 3–0 lead on a two-run single by Connor and a sacrifice fly by Dante. Mike held the Tigers in check, giving up a long double to the Tigers' cleanup hitter in the top of the third inning before ending the threat with two strikeouts in a row.

With the bottom of the Orioles order due up, Coach said, "Marty, go warm up Cody."

"See that?!" Marty crowed, grabbing a catcher's mitt and face mask. "Coach knows who to put in charge of the rookie right-hander!"

Cody warmed up down the left-field line. His hands were sweaty and he could feel his heart thumping. He couldn't remember ever being this jittery on a baseball field. His first two throws sailed over Marty's head. The third bounced so hard it nearly dug a divot at Marty's feet.

"Whoa!" he said. "Hey, Tim Lincecum! Maybe we could try not to hit one hundred on the radar gun until you're actually facing a batter!"

Cody nodded and took a deep breath. Hoo, boy, he thought. This was going to be . . . *interesting*.

It was still 3–0 Orioles when, in the top of the fourth inning, Cody walked stiffly to the mound for his pitching debut.

He took his warm-up tosses and was relieved to see that none of them ended up in the Tigers' dugout. After the last one, Joey fired the ball down to Connor at second base and jogged out to the mound.

"Got a few butterflies in the stomach?" the stocky

catcher asked. He was chomping on his usual four pieces of bubble gum, a wad that stuck out like a golf ball in his cheek.

"They feel more like bats flapping around," Cody said, rubbing the ball furiously.

Joey nodded, blowing a huge bubble.

"We'll keep this real simple," he said. "I put down one finger. You throw a fastball. That's all you gotta remember, okay?"

Cody nodded and thought: a kid who gets a 98 on his social studies test ought to be able to handle that.

As the first batter dug in at the plate, the Tigers' dugout erupted with catcalls.

"Big, *big* man on the mound!"

"I can't believe I ate the whole thing!"

"Yo, pitcher! Grand Slam breakfast at Denny's! Available twenty-four/seven!"

Cody could feel the familiar anger rising as the Tigers batter dug in. Anger and adrenaline—that's a bad combination, he told himself. He went into his windup, kicked, rocked, and fired. Ball one. He threw the second pitch even harder. Ball two. Great, he thought. The kid hasn't moved the bat from his shoulders. And why should he? He's taking the E-ZPass lane to first base.

Cody walked the kid on two more balls outside. And the next batter walked on four pitches too. Now the Tigers' dugout was a sea of noise, the jeering getting louder and louder. Cody ran the count to 2–0 on the third batter when Coach yelled, "Time!" and popped out of the dugout.

He trudged slowly to the mound while Cody kicked

nervously at the dirt in front of the pitching rubber.

"Cody," Coach said, "look at me."

Cody tilted his head up slightly.

"You can do this," Coach said. "Don't let these guys get to you. All you need to do is find your rhythm, and you'll be fine."

"I don't know, Coach," Cody said, looking down and kicking the dirt again.

"Well, I *do* know," Coach said. The irritation in his voice startled Cody. "But you're not giving yourself a chance. And you're not giving your teammates a chance to help you. Now take a deep breath and relax. Then take ten miles per hour off that fastball and get it over the plate. I don't want to have to come out here again." With that, he turned and left.

Cody tried to compose himself. *Breathe. Relax. Slow everything down.* And he did. Slowed everything down so much it was like he was taking a nap. The result was a pitch that seemed to float through the air as the batter's eyes lit up with delight. The kid promptly slapped it into right-center field for a two-run double.

Just like that, it was Orioles 3, Tigers 2.

Cody was furious with himself. *Why don't I just throw it underhand if I'm going to pitch that slow? Why don't I bowl it up there?*

He tried throwing the ball slightly harder now, and suddenly his luck seemed to change. The next Tigers batter swung at a pitch outside the strike zone and hit a weak comebacker to the mound for the first out. The batter after that helped Cody even more by striking out on a fastball over his head. And the Tigers' number-nine hitter swung at three balls in the dirt to end the inning.

Cody hung his head as he walked off the mound. Some debut. Then he said a silent prayer: I don't know what those last three guys were swinging at. But please don't let them stop swinging at junk now.

When he reached the dugout, Coach gave him a fist-bump and said, "Okay, not bad. You got out of trouble when you had to." But Cody was disconsolate. What a train-wreck of an outing, he thought.

Which was when Marty walked over and put a hand on each shoulder and got right in his face.

"Listen to me, dude," Marty said. "Forget that big windup of yours. It's killing you. You're totally off balance. Just pitch from the stretch, like the closers in the major leagues do. It'll make your delivery way more compact. You'll have much better control."

Cody's jaw dropped. Marty, the kid who talked to himself, the kid who couldn't run to first base without stumbling, was talking like a big-league pitching coach. And the scary thing was, he was actually making sense.

"Okay," Cody said, nodding. "Why not? I'm not exactly mowing them down this way."

So when he took the mound in the fifth inning, Cody pitched from the stretch. And something clicked immediately. He could feel it in his warm-up throws. He wasn't teetering all over the place. Everything seemed so much smoother. Every pitch was around the plate, even when he threw hard. Joey didn't have to make one sprawling kick save.

With his newfound confidence, Cody set the Tigers down in order. The first batter grounded out to Jordy at first. The next batter hit a pop foul near the Tigers' dugout that Jordy also gloved. Cody's fastball was popping into Joey's mitt. And the next batter—the Tigers' number-three hitter—struck out to end the inning.

This time Cody sprinted off the mound with a big smile on his face, accepting fist bumps from his teammates as he neared the dugout. Marty stood on the top step grinning like a proud parent.

"You're a genius!" Cody said, wrapping the skinny kid in a bear hug.

"There are those who think so," Marty said, shrugging. "Who am I to argue?"

The Orioles were still clinging to a 3–2 lead when Cody took the mound for the sixth inning. But he was in a groove now. The Tigers' cleanup hitter, a big kid named Manny, hit a fly ball to deep center field that scared Cody—until Yancy ran it down for the first out.

But Cody got the Tigers' number-five hitter on a slow grounder to second base. And when he fanned the next batter on three straight fastballs for the Orioles' seventh straight win, Joey pumped his fist and ran out to high-five his pitcher, touching off a small celebration near the mound.

"Way to close it out," Coach said, beaming. "I knew you had it in you."

"*I* didn't," Cody said, shaking his head. "But you were right about me not relying enough on the rest of the guys. Thanks, Coach."

After the two teams lined up and slapped hands, Willie pretended to interview Cody, holding his fist out like it was a microphone and he was a TV sideline reporter.

"We're talking with one of the stars of today's game, Orioles relief pitcher Cody Parker," Willie began. "Cody, terrific outing. What was working for you out there?"

"Well, I felt good today," Cody said, playing along perfectly. All those hours of watching ESPN *SportsCenter* had actually paid off. "I was locating my pitches real well, changing speeds, able to keep the hitters off balance."

Willie nodded earnestly. "Now, I know you hadn't pitched in quite a few years," he continued. "That must have been a little nerve-racking, moving from third base to the bullpen on such short notice."

"I just want to help the team," Cody said. "Whatever they want me to do is fine with me. The bottom line is, I just want to help us win a ring."

"They don't give rings in this league, Cody," Willie said with a straight face. "They only give you a trophy if you win the championship. And it's not very big, either."

Cody tried not to crack up. "Rings, trophies, it's all the same to me," he said. "I'm all about the team."

"Well, there you have it," Willie said, pretending to turn to an imaginary camera. "A young phenom came of age today. Cody Parker closes out the Tigers in a thrilling three to two Orioles win. Now back to you guys in the booth."

With the "interview" over, the rest of the Orioles burst out laughing. Willie and Cody slapped hands and laughed too. For Cody, it had pretty much been a perfect day. But as he gathered up his stuff and said good-bye to his teammates, he had the eerie feeling that someone was watching him. Turning around, he saw Dante standing by the corner of the dugout, glowering at him.

"You think you're pretty funny, don't you, fat boy?" he said. He spit out a mouthful of sunflower seeds and nodded grimly. Without another word, he slung his equipment bag over his shoulder and stomped off into the twilight.

"What's his problem?" Willie said as they stared at the retreating figure.

"Apparently it's me," Cody said. "Which makes it my problem too."

Cody took two dribbles to his right, until he was almost behind the basket, and then he put up a fifteen-foot rainbow while nearly brushing against the garage door. He held his follow-through with his right hand extended high in the air, like the best shooters in the NBA and college. *Swish*. He grinned, retrieved the ball, and fired a bounce pass to Jessica.

"No way you'll make that shot," he said. "You don't have that kind of talent."

Jessica snorted and waved dismissively. "Are you kidding?" she said, dribbling over to where Cody had let the ball fly. "I make this shot in my sleep."

She took a deep breath and launched a jumper. The ball clanged noisily off the front of the rim and rolled into the hedge. They both looked at each other and laughed.

They were playing H-O-R-S-E in Jessica's driveway, one day after the Orioles' big win over the Tigers, and she was down to her last letter. One more miss and Cody would be the winner.

"This is where I excel," Cody said, dribbling out to the top of the key. "Nailing down the win. Hitting the tough shot. Putting unbelievable pressure on my opponent."

Jessica rolled her eyes. "I know one thing," she said. "You're putting unbelievable pressure on your mouth with your lips flapping like that."

Both of them were pretty good at trash talk. That was half the fun of the game, seeing if you could get under the other player's skin or make them laugh to throw off their shot.

Cody dribbled between his legs and put up a seventeen-footer. *Swish*. Jessica groaned as she retrieved the ball.

"I can't believe how lucky you are," she said.

"Luck has nothing to do with it," Cody said. "It's all about natural athletic ability. And an incredible laserlike focus. Not to mention a burning will to win."

"Puh-leeze," Jessica said, blowing a stray lock of hair out of her eyes as she readied to shoot. "Now you're making me nauseous."

This time her shot bounced off the back of the rim and caromed into Mrs. Hoffman's flower bed.

Cody shouted, "Yessss!" pumped his fist, and danced wildly around the driveway.

"Well," Jessica said, shaking her head, "at least you're a classy winner. At least you're not rubbing it in."

"It's hard to be humble when you're me," Cody said, nodding and holding his arms aloft, as if acknowledging the roars of a crowd. "Someone who wants the ball in pressure situations. Someone with ice water in his veins."

"There must be at least one sports cliché you haven't

used this afternoon," Jessica said. "But I sure can't think of it."

"Admit it. The chunkster's got game," Cody said.

"You're not the chunkster anymore," Jessica said. "Looks like you lost a few pounds, Wisconsin Boy."

Cody felt himself blush and hoped Jessica didn't notice. They kept shooting baskets even after the game was over, enjoying the last of the warm afternoon sun. They talked about school and Cody's baseball team and Jessica's softball team and her karate lessons.

"Been meaning to ask," Jessica said. "What's going on with Dante? Is he still bothering you?"

Now Cody wore a pained look. "You had to bring him up, huh?" he said. "And here we were having such a good time."

"Sorry," Jessica said. "Guess the answer is yes."

"Dante still wants to punch my lights out, if that's what you mean," Cody said. "He's still as friendly as a crocodile."

Quickly, he filled her in on the events of the previous day, including the older boy's sarcastic comment about Cody's mock interview with Willie and the semi-threat he had made after the Orioles win.

"I'm not afraid of him," Cody said, plopping down on the Hoffman's lawn. He glanced sheepishly at Jessica. "Okay, I'm a *little* afraid. Guess I have to stand up to him, though. Unless I hire you to be my security detail."

"You can't afford my rates," Jessica said, spinning and delivering a kick to an imaginary foe. Then she grinned. "I start at five hundred bucks an hour. But since we're friends, I'd cut you a break. Only four ninety-nine."

"Gee, thanks," Cody said. But even that little joke couldn't cheer him up. "Why does he hate me so much, anyway?"

"Not sure," Jessica said, sitting down next to him. "But he's an angry kid. I hear he lives with his mom, who works all hours. His brothers are always pushing him around. All they do is skip school and hang out in the park bothering people. I'm surprised Dante still plays baseball—maybe it's to get away from them."

She pulled up a tuft of grass and idly tossed it in the air.

"My advice, Wisconsin Boy," she continued, "is to just stay away from him. You don't want to get into a fight with him. He's bigger than you, he's older than you . . ."

Her voice trailed off, then she shook her head emphatically. "I don't think that would go too well for the Orioles' newest relief pitcher," she added. "Maybe Dante'll get bored with you and start picking on someone else."

It reminded Cody of the conversation he'd had at lunch earlier that day with Willie, Jordy, and Connor. Weeks ago, Cody had confided in them about the trouble he'd been having with Dante. But when he'd sat down with them today and told them he was tired of being bullied and was thinking of confronting Dante to make it stop, they had all looked at him as if he'd lost his mind.

"Dude, he'll pound you like a bad piece of meat," Jordy had said.

"Break you into little pieces," Connor had added.

"Yeah," Willie had said, "then break *those* little pieces into little pieces."

"Thanks for the vote of confidence," Cody had said glumly, taking a bite of his sandwich.

"Plus, don't forget the Rottweiler Twins," Jordy had added. "Even if, by some miracle, you manage to get Dante to back down, he'll sic his crazy brothers on you."

But sitting here now with Jessica, as twilight descended and the first chirping of crickets could be heard, Cody had already made up his mind. It was time to stand up to the big guy.

"I have a plan. . . ." Cody said now. Jessica was sitting with her knees curled under her chin, rocking back and forth, and now she looked up.

"Actually, it's something my dad thought up," Cody continued. "And by the way? It's designed to help me *not* get my butt whipped."

He explained the plan to Jessica exactly as it had been explained to him, beginning with the three sentences his dad had scribbled on the napkin in the restaurant near Camden Yards.

When he was through, Jessica was silent. She sat there with her brow furrowed, looking off into the distance, as if considering all the ramifications of what Cody had just proposed.

Well, he thought, at least she's not doubled over with laughter. At least she didn't blurt out, "Wow, that might be the stupidest thing I ever heard!" That was encouraging—sort of.

Finally, Jessica nodded almost imperceptibly. "You know," she said, "it just might work. In fact, seeing how Dante reacted when I kicked him with all the kids watching, I'd say it *will* work."

Hearing this, Cody felt relieved. The two of them climbed

to their feet and exchanged a fist bump.

"When will you try out this so-called plan?" Jessica asked.

"Tomorrow," Cody said. "Right after school. I've put it off long enough."

Cody awoke before dawn the next morning, unable to get back to sleep. He had tossed and turned for much of the night, finding it nearly impossible to shut off his brain as dozens of different "what if" scenarios ran through his head.

What if this crazy plan of his dad's didn't work? What if all it did was make Dante even angrier? What if the big guy decided to whack him like a piñata right then and there? Good luck sending up a Bat-Signal to Jessica.

No, in a cruel bit of irony, Jessica would be at her karate class by 2:45. And what could she do even if she knew Cody was getting pummeled? Raise her hand and say, "Sensei, may I be excused to go save my not-so-chubby friend from Milwaukee again?"

Not so chubby—that doesn't sound bad, Cody thought. Even in his wired state, it made him smile.

All morning in school, he could barely pay attention. In Ms. Wratched's science class, he completely zoned out. Part of that had to do with Ms. Wratched, who spoke in a low, droning monotone and who had been deemed the

Most Boring Teacher Ever by much of the eighth grade. But part of it was Cody's out-of-control imagination, which kept picturing Dante's fist crashing into his face like some kind of killer asteroid.

At lunch, Cody plopped down next to Jordy, Connor, and Willie at their usual table.

"I have an announcement," Cody said, rustling through his lunch bag. "Today is D-day. And you know who the D stands for."

Three pairs of eyebrows shot up at once.

"Dude, didn't we go over this?" Jordy said. "Didn't we say he'll pound you like a—"

"Bad piece of meat. I know, I know . . ." Cody said. He shook his head firmly. "It's still D-day."

His three friends looked at one another with alarm.

"Will you talk to the boy?" Willie said to Connor. "Tell him he's not just walking into the jaws of death, he's sprinting?"

Connor started to speak, but Cody held up a hand.

"I don't intend to get my butt whupped," he said. "Sure, it *could* happen. But I'm hoping to use psychology."

"Psychology," Willie repeated. He looked incredulously at Jordy and Connor, then back to Cody. "How about if Dante uses physics? Such as Newton's Third Law: for every action, there's an equal and opposite reaction? Like, you come near him and he punches your lights out?"

Cody gulped. But he tried to keep his voice even.

"I think I'll be okay," he said, taking a bite of an apple. "Besides, look what I'm eating now instead of cookies. Getting in fighting shape!"

Hearing himself talk so boldly about a showdown with Dante, Cody felt like the proverbial kid whistling past a graveyard. But there was no sense getting into the details of his plan right now. Or when he would execute it. His buddies wouldn't understand. Or they'd think he was nuts and try to talk him out of it.

Soon the conversation shifted away from Dante to a new video game, *Wipeout on 64th St.*, where the hero surfer navigated his board through a grim urban obstacle course filled with menacing villains. Cody sighed and looked out the window. Even though it was a warm sunny day, he felt a shiver go through him. Wish the only thing I had to worry about was video game bad guys, he thought. At that moment, he felt like the loneliest kid on the planet.

The rest of the afternoon seemed to crawl by even more slowly than the morning had. Social studies was Cody's favorite subject. But when Miss Brock stood in front of the class and said, "Who can name three ways the people of sub-Saharan Africa have adapted to their environment?" Cody's mind was a blank. As he glanced at the clock on the wall, he could feel himself getting more and more nervous. He noticed his legs were jiggling furiously too.

When the final bell rang at 2:30, he weaved through the crowded hallways to his locker, then joined the rest of the kids pouring out the front doors into the bright sunshine. But instead of veering off to catch his bus as he usually did, he crossed the street and headed for the grassy knoll on the other side.

Up ahead, he saw a knot of kids chattering away excitedly as they said good-bye to friends before beginning the walk home. Cody's school bus passed here every afternoon, and he knew this was the route Dante took too, often accompanied by one or two of his thuggish friends.

Seconds later, he spotted Dante, with his head down, checking his cell phone. Technically, you weren't allowed to use your cell anywhere on school property. But Cody knew the big guy didn't worry about little things like rules and regulations.

When Dante looked up and saw Cody walking toward him, he seemed surprised. Then he flashed his trademark sneer.

"Fat boy!" he said. "What are you doing here? And where's your bodyguard? You give her the day off?"

The two older kids with Dante laughed nervously. Cody sensed they seemed unsure of exactly what their leader was referring to but apparently felt obligated to react to his sarcasm.

"You're even dumber than I thought, coming over here," Dante continued, his voice louder now. Hearing this, a few of the kids who had been walking up ahead turned around, sensing some sort of trouble that might turn into their afternoon entertainment.

Slowly, Dante peeled off his backpack and flung it dramatically to the ground. "I've been waiting for this," he said, balling his fists and taking a step forward.

Cody's heart was racing. His hands were sweating. He took a deep breath.

"Showtime," he whispered to himself.

What happened next felt like one long blur.

"AAAGGGHHH!" he shouted at the top of his lungs,

running at Dante and getting inches from his face.

Then Cody began jerking his head back and forth and wagging his tongue and rolling his eyeballs. He threw himself to the ground, grunting and spinning in circles like a break-dancer before popping to his feet and hissing loudly.

Dante backed up, a look of confusion on his face. His two buddies watched, bug-eyed.

"Porker," Dante said, "just what do you think you're do—"

Next Cody started drooling and stamping his feet to go along with the rest of his contortions.

"Throw in a bark or two," his dad had said. So Cody barked and howled like some kind of unholy hound from the netherworld. Then he bared his teeth and raised his fingers like claws and growled ferociously.

I'll either win an Academy Award for this or get flattened in the next three seconds, he thought.

"Whoa!" he heard someone in the background say. And now the entire knot of kids seemed to gasp and take a step back.

Dante stood there, frozen. He stared ashen-faced at Cody for what seemed like thirty seconds. Then he slowly reached down and began feeling around for his backpack, his eyes never leaving Cody.

"Ohhh-kay, Parker," he said softly. "I have to go now. Why don't you just—?"

"GRRRRR!" Cody growled, giving him one more for good measure.

Dante jumped as if he'd just been shocked. He grabbed his backpack, stood up, and backed away. When he was about six feet away, he turned and ran, sprinting up the hill with his two henchmen in tow, the three of them glancing nervously over their shoulders.

Seeing that the show was over, the rest of the kids began drifting away. Cody slumped against a tree, trying to catch his breath. His heart was hammering in his chest, and his legs were shaking. How did the movie stars do it? This kind of intense acting was exhausting! Of course, the movie stars probably weren't worried about getting punched out by a cranky bully if they didn't nail the scene.

Then he heard someone running up behind him. Could it be Dante again? Had the big guy been playing possum? Cody whirled around.

It was Jessica.

"That was awesome!" she said, grinning.

Now it was Cody's turn to look shocked. But the shock quickly gave way to major embarrassment. Had she seen his whole crazy, saliva-spewing act? How uncool was that?

"What are *you* doing here?!" he asked.

Jessica shrugged. "Thought you might need help," she said. "I'd miss ten more karate classes just to see that look on Dante's face again."

They heard the sound of footsteps coming up the hill, and Willie, Jordy, and Connor came flying over the crest.

"Dude, where *were* you?" Willie said, gasping for breath.

"Yeah," Jordy said. "We thought your little showdown with Dante would happen right outside school."

"Kinda hard to have your back way up here on Mount Everest," Connor said. "So, what happened?"

Jessica gave them a quick recap of the confrontation,

complete with Cody's all-star impression of a disturbed person and Dante's wide-eyed flight, which caused everyone to laugh. Then she draped an arm around Cody and said, "You did real well, Wisconsin Boy."

Cody could feel his face redden. But inside he felt proud.

"Wish I could take all the credit," he said.

With that, he pulled an old, crumpled napkin out of his pants pocket and unfolded it until they could read the three sentences his dad had written:

Act like a crazy person. Bullies don't know how to handle crazy people. And they hate to be embarrassed in front of others.

Cody shook his head and smiled. By tomorrow word might be spreading throughout York Middle that the fat kid from Wisconsin was certifiably psycho. But if it kept Dante from terrorizing him, it was worth it, he thought.

Oh, Dante might still hate his guts. And the Rottweiler Twins might be lurking somewhere down the road. But Cody had a feeling Dante himself wouldn't be bothering him anymore.

It would sure be a nice change. And knowing his new friends cared so much about him made him feel even better.

"C'mon," he said to the four of them. "I'll buy you an ice cream to celebrate."

"Better make it frozen yogurt," Jessica said, grinning and poking him in the belly. "The nonfat kind."

15

The question caught Cody off guard. One minute he had stopped in the Orioles' dugout for a quick drink of Gatorade, the next minute he was practically spitting a stream of the stuff across the cement floor, like people did on the sitcoms when they were startled.

"Why do you talk to your bat?" Marty repeated.

The Orioles were warming up now, getting ready to play the Blue Jays at Eddie Murray Field on a damp evening that was unusually chilly for late May. Nevertheless, Cody could feel his face getting hot from embarrassment.

"Is it for, like, good luck or something?" Marty pressed.

Cody was relieved to see there was no one else in the dugout. He glanced up at Marty to see if the kid was messing with him. But Marty seemed genuinely curious.

Cody tried to think of the right thing to say. After he had flipped out on Dante, there had been whispers in school that Cody might be a head case. Luckily, the rumors had stopped by now—Jordy, Willie, and Connor had spread the word that it was all an act designed to get Dante to leave him alone. And as Cody had predicted, Dante hadn't come

93

near him since. Oh, he was still giving Cody dirty looks from a distance. But whenever the big guy saw Cody and Jessica together, he seemed to recoil, as if terrified that both a wacko and a martial artist might descend upon him.

Still, the last thing Cody needed now was for kids to start calling him the Bat Whisperer or something. Like that dumb old movie his mom had about the guy who talked to horses.

"I don't know what you're talking about," he said at last, snorting. "C'mon, who talks to their bat?"

"You do," Marty said matter-of-factly. He reached into his back pocket and pulled out a package of sunflower seeds. "I saw you do it the first time you took batting practice with us."

Marty shook some seeds into his mouth and chewed, staring at Cody the whole time. Within seconds, Cody found it unnerving. Boy, he thought, if Dad ever needs somebody to sweat one of the bad guys during an interrogation, Marty's his man.

Marty kept chewing and staring, chewing and staring. Cody looked away, pretending to be fascinated with a crack in the dugout wall as he finished his drink. The muffled sounds of the Orioles and Blue Jays warming up, of baseballs plunking into soft leather and pinging off aluminum bats, drifted into the dugout. Otherwise, the only sound was the soft *crunch, crunch, crunch* of Marty's teeth grinding the seeds.

After about ninety seconds, Cody cracked.

"Okay, fine," he said, throwing up his hands. "I'll admit that I do—*occasionally*—whisper a little something to my bat. And, yes, it's for good luck. But it's no big deal. I'm not a wack job or anything."

Marty nodded thoughtfully and continued chewing. The answer seemed to satisfy him. He folded the packet of seeds and placed it carefully back in his pocket.

"I talk to lots of things," he said. "I talk to the ball when I'm in the outfield. My glove too. I talk to my dog, of course. And my fish."

Cody stood and grabbed his glove, ready to get back to warming up. This was getting weird. Mad weird.

"Mainly I talk to things because people don't always listen to me," Marty continued. "I don't know if you've noticed, but they think I'm kind of odd."

Cody tried hard to suppress a smile. He drained the last of his Gatorade and tossed the cup in the trash can.

"You? Odd?" he said. "I don't get that at all. C'mon, let's go play catch."

He picked up a ball and tossed it at Marty. Marty grinned and grabbed his glove.

As they trotted out to the field, Marty said, "Oh, and Cody?"

"Yeah?"

"Don't worry. I won't tell anyone you talk to your bat."

"Thanks," Cody said, punching him playfully on the shoulder. "That would be a big help."

Fifteen minutes later, Coach called them together. Quickly he ran through the lineup that would take the field against the Blue Jays. Then he hitched up his belt, tugged his cap low over his eyes, and cleared his throat. The Orioles looked at one another. A major Coach speech was coming. Possibly even a State of the Orioles address.

"Guys," he said, "we're having an outstanding season. We're 11–0 right now. And you should be very proud of yourselves. Does anyone remember what I said at one of our very first practices?"

No one raised a hand.

"About this team's potential?" Coach said. "Anyone?"

Still no hands. The silence was deafening.

Coach sighed and shook his head softly. "I'm glad to see my words leave such a lasting impression on all of you," he said. "What I said was that this team has the potential to—"

"OOOH! OOOH!" a voice cried. Marty's hand shot into the air. He was wriggling like a worm.

"Marty?" Coach said.

"You said we had a great shot to become the best in the league," Marty said. "You said we could even go undefeated."

"Exactly," Coach said. Marty beamed as if he had just aced his Pre-algebra final.

"It's all up to you, men," Coach continued. "The play-offs begin next week. An undefeated season would be something special. Something you'd remember for the rest of your lives."

The Orioles were nodding now. Connor and Jordy slapped high fives. Willie pounded his fist into his glove and murmured, "Yeah!" Robbie and Yancy banged their bats against the bench. Marty was up and dancing. Even Dante had exchanged his usual scowl for something that resembled—well, almost—a smile.

Cody had to give Coach credit. He sure knew how to get a team fired up.

"All right, hands in the middle," Coach said as the team surrounded him. "We all know what the goal is now. Let's get started on it today."

"One-two-three, Orioles!" they yelled.

Robbie struck out the first Blue Jays batter, got the second one on a weak grounder back to the mound, and struck out the third one to end the inning. He was pumped, throwing hard but under control, and his fastball was popping into Joey's mitt.

"Let's jump on them right away!" Connor said as the Orioles hustled off the field.

"All right!" Coach said, fist-bumping Robbie. "Time for Murderers' Row to get cranking!"

But Murderers' Row could have stayed home in bed—at least for this inning. The Blue Jays' pitcher was a short, hefty kid named Kyle Mattison, who also happened to be in Cody's gym class. Usually, he had an excellent changeup, one of the best in the league, according to Coach. But the Orioles could see the kid was struggling even with his warm-up pitches. He was having trouble keeping them in the same area code, never mind getting them over the plate.

Willie led things off with a walk on four pitches. With Robbie up, he promptly stole second on the next pitch, despite a great throw by the Blue Jays' catcher. On the next pitch, he caught the Blue Jays napping and stole third without a throw, since Kyle failed to hold him and the third baseman forgot to cover the bag.

"This is why I feel like a genius!" Marty hooted. "Willie's only the fastest kid in the league! How do you forget about the fastest kid in the league when he's on base?!"

And Willie wasn't through yet. The Orioles could tell, just by watching his body language. He took a big lead off third, rocking back and forth, one foot to the other, a coiled bundle of energy.

"He's gone on the next pitch," Yancy murmured.

This time, though, Willie had Kyle's full attention. The Jays pitcher threw over to third once, twice, three times. Willie dove safely back each time. And each time he popped up grinning and dusting himself off.

After the third throw over, the Orioles began crooning the theme music from *Jeopardy*, the one that was played at major league ballparks whenever there was a conference on the mound and it looked like the visiting team was stalling for time.

"Doo-doo-doo-doo, doo-doo-doo . . ." they sang, drawing a glare from Kyle.

After yet another futile attempt to pick off Willie, Kyle seemed resigned to his fate. He peered in for the signal from his catcher, came to the stretch position, and reared back. Willie was off.

"HE'S GOING!" the entire Blue Jays infield screamed.

But it was too late. Kyle tried to hurry his delivery, but that only made things worse. He lunged awkwardly on his left foot and the pitch bounced in the dirt. The Jays catcher did a great job of blocking it, but couldn't come up with the ball as Willie slid across the plate in a cloud of dust.

"He's safe!" the umpire cried.

Just like that, it was 1–0 Orioles. And not one of the Orioles had even lifted the bat from his shoulder yet.

From there things only got worse for Kyle. He walked Robbie, Jordy doubled him home, and Connor followed with another RBI double. Unnerved now, Kyle tried to blow the ball past Cody and ended up walking him on four pitches. Then Dante singled Connor home to make it 4–0 Orioles.

Taking his lead off second base, Cody felt sorry for Kyle. The kid was sweating as if he'd just climbed out of a sauna even though the temperature had dropped another ten degrees. Cody knew how lonely it was on the mound when things were going badly, and your legs felt like rubber, and you didn't have a clue as to where the ball was going.

When Yancy walked yet again to load the bases, the Blue Jays' coach finally called time and trudged out to replace his pitcher. Cody silently applauded as he jogged to third. About time, Coach, he thought. Give the kid a break.

Kyle did a slow death march back to the dugout with his head down, fighting back tears. But the next Blue Jays pitcher didn't do much better, and neither did the one after that. It was one of those days when the Orioles could do no wrong as they belted out twelve hits to accompany all their walks, ending in a thorough butt-whipping of their opponent.

Final score: Orioles 11, Blue Jays 0. It was their twelfth straight win. And they seemed to be peaking at exactly the right time, with the play-offs just around the corner.

As they lined up and slapped hands with the Jays, Cody made it a point to talk to Kyle, whose eyes were still red-rimmed.

"Tough one," he said softly.

"Tell me about it," Kyle said with a rueful smile.

"But you'll be back," Cody said. "Our coach said you have the best changeup in the whole league."

Kyle seemed to brighten. "He did? Thanks." As the Blue Jays walked back to their dugout, Cody noticed that Kyle's shoulders sagged a little less now.

What a game this is, Cody thought. One minute it can make you feel great. The next minute it can make you want to lock yourself in your room for a week.

Listen to me, he thought. A little baseball philosophy from the Bat Whisperer himself.

Cody loved Coach Mike's class. Physical education instructor Michael Theodore Lombardi was by far the oldest faculty member at York Middle. His students delighted in speculating about his age, with the guesses ranging from sixty to eighty to already dead.

His waxy gray skin stretched like parchment over his gaunt six-foot-one frame, and when he wore his ancient Chuck Taylor sneakers and a tight T-shirt and gym shorts that reached only to his skinny thighs, it was like seeing a character from a documentary about phys ed in the old days come to life.

Long ago Coach Mike had arrived at the conclusion that he could no longer remember the names of his fellow teachers, never mind the students. When this realization hit, he made the decision to simplify his professional life and not worry about names at all. Instead, he began calling everyone Chief, even the women and girls.

Another distinguishing characteristic of Coach Mike was that he invariably ended each instruction to his students with the word *'kay?*, for "Okay?"

"Today we're going to play some badminton, 'kay?" he'd announce. "We'll divide up into ten teams, 'kay? Each game to eleven points, 'kay? Winning team stays on the court, 'kay?"

This distinctive style of speaking was endlessly parodied by Cody's class, who would automatically lapse into "Lombardi speak" the moment they passed through the gym doors. Soon, all twenty-five of them would be jabbering like their teacher and calling each other Chief and cracking up. As for Coach Mike, he remained clueless the whole time.

Cody always looked forward to Coach Mike's class because he wasn't like the tough-guy, no-nonsense gym teachers Cody had had in the past. He wasn't always telling you to tuck in your shirt and pull up your shorts, for one thing. And he didn't care if you didn't do things exactly right in his class, like demonstrate perfect form when serving in volleyball, the unit they were on now.

On the Monday following the Orioles' big win over the Blue Jays, Cody's volleyball team was about to take the court when Cody ran to his locker to get a different pair of sneakers. When he returned, he was frowning.

"Coach Mike," he said, "my cell phone is missing."

"You're talking about your portable phone, Chief?" Coach Mike asked.

Cody nodded. He forgot Coach Mike wasn't exactly up on the latest technology. If any of the kids ever tried talking to him about laptops or iPads or smartphones, he would wave his hands and bark impatiently, "I don't know anything about that stuff! And guess what? I don't wanna know!"

"It was in my locker five minutes ago," Cody said. "Now it's gone."

Coach Mike sighed and ran a thin, bony hand through the few remaining strands of hair on his head. "Obvious question," he said. "Was your locker locked?"

"Yeah," Cody said. "I'm pretty sure it was."

"And you looked everywhere?"

Cody resisted the temptation to say: "Well, if I looked *everywhere*, I would have already found it." Instead, he simply nodded. He had searched the pockets of his clothes, his backpack, his locker, and even the other unlocked lockers nearby.

Coach rubbed his chin and stared down at the floor, as if giving the matter a great deal of thought. Finally, he shrugged. "I'm sure it'll turn up somewhere," he said. "We'll look for it after class. Might as well get back to your game."

Cody was worried about his phone, but playing volleyball helped take his mind off of it. He was pretty good at volleyball, even for a big kid. He had a sneaky game at the net, where he would often fake a kill shot and then dink the ball over the net for a point. And he'd noticed that he felt lighter these days. He was able to jump higher than ever before, which allowed him to slam the ball even more effectively.

The only weird thing about today's volleyball game was that Dante was on his team. The big dude still hadn't said a word to him since Cody had gone psycho on him. Most of the time Dante wouldn't look at him even when they were sitting near each other in the Orioles' dugout.

It made for some strange moments. In the fifth inning

against the Blue Jays, when Cody had returned to the dugout after driving in a run with a long sacrifice fly, all the Orioles had stood to greet him with their hands up for high fives.

Dante had joined his teammates—Coach would have jumped on him if he hadn't. But when Cody slapped hands with Dante, Dante stared down at his spikes. After that, he quickly moved to the far end of the dugout.

"I see you're still not on Dante's Christmas-card list," Willie had whispered after watching his behavior.

"No, he loves me," Cody had whispered back. "The big lug just doesn't know how to show it."

Still, being ignored by Dante was fine with Cody—far better than having to worry about Dante swooping out from behind a car and giving him another gravel bath, or stalking him after he got off the school bus.

But Cody's mind was on volleyball now, and the class seemed to fly by. The two teams were evenly matched, and late in the final decisive game, the score was tied at 9–9, with players on both teams whooping and cheering after every point.

Which was exactly when Nicky Evans, a short, chubby kid on Cody's team, decided he had to go to the bathroom.

"Now?" Coach Mike said. "The game's almost over! And class is over in a few minutes!"

Nicky looked at him with pleading eyes, clutching his stomach.

Coach Mike threw up his hands in frustration and said, "Okay, okay, when you gotta go, you gotta go."

A girl named Vanessa offered to take Nicky's place, and

the game continued, just as spirited as before. It ended with a tall boy named Javier slamming the winning point for Cody's team, touching off a wild round of celebrating and trash talk from the victors.

As the boys trooped into the locker room, Coach Mike bellowed, "After you change, everyone take a moment to look around for Cody's portable phone, please!"

"It's the twenty-first century! They call them cell phones now, Coach Mike!" a few kids yelled. As always, Coach Mike pretended not to hear.

Suddenly, Nicky emerged from behind a row of lockers with a pained expression on his face.

"Stomach still acting up, Chief?" Coach Mike said.

"Worse than that!" Nicky said breathlessly. "My cell's missing too! My mom's going to kill me!"

Coach Mike put his hands on his hips and stared at Nicky for several seconds. Then he slowly swiveled his head from side to side, his watery eyes taking in the entire room.

"What in God's name is going on here?" he said. "Two portable phones missing in one class? Well, they didn't just grow legs, people! They have to be here someplace!"

But they weren't. The boys went up and down each aisle, opening and closing lockers and even searching under the benches, on top of shelves, and in the hallway. Nothing turned up.

By this point, Nicky seemed on the verge of tears.

Suddenly, Dante raised his hand.

"Coach Mike, there was a kid snooping around here earlier," he said. "He was opening and closing lockers. I saw him when I came in to change."

He dropped his voice to a dramatic hush. "And he's right here with us."

The room was absolutely still now. The boys exchanged uneasy glances, then turned back to Dante, who seemed to be enjoying his moment in the spotlight.

"Okay, Chief, this isn't *Law and Order*," Coach Mike barked. "Get on with it! Who was it?"

Dante smiled mysteriously. For a second or two, he said nothing. Then he whirled around and pointed at Cody.

"It was him!" he said.

Now all eyes turned to Cody, who stood gaping with astonishment.

"WHAT?!" he cried. "Are you crazy?"

Dante shrugged and looked away. Coach Mike looked around the locker room, seemingly lost in thought. Just then the bell rang.

"No," Coach said at last, looking at Cody. "Why would the boy tell me his own phone was stolen if he was the one doing the stealing? Doesn't make any sense. Fellas, I suggest you report this to the office. You watch. Those phones'll turn up somewhere."

He clapped Nicky on the back and said, "Cheer up, Chief. It's not the end of the world."

"No," Nicky said mournfully, slipping on his backpack. "But it might be the end of me."

The cafeteria was even noisier than usual, three days later—so loud it was almost giving Cody a headache. In addition to the usual lunchtime pandemonium of trays clattering and coins clanging into vending machines and paper bags rustling, it seemed every kid in the place was yakking away at a decibel level that rivaled a Justin Bieber concert.

"Let me guess," Cody said dryly, tossing his lunch bag on the table. "Everyone's talking about the big food drive to help the homeless."

Willie looked around and shrugged. "You gotta admit it's pretty exciting," he said. "It's not every day you have the police crawling all over the place and students being questioned."

Cody nodded. Willie was right—you couldn't blame the kids. "The Great York Middle Crime Wave," as it had been dubbed, was all anyone was talking about.

Even though there had been a few thefts in previous weeks, most of the school considered the start of the crime wave to be the day Cody and Nicky Evans had reported their cell phones missing in gym class. Later that same day, a girl in eighth grade had reported that her cell had been stolen from her locker.

By the next morning, a computer from the computer lab was missing, and two teachers had reported having their wallets stolen from their handbags. And just the day before, Ms. Wratched had arrived at school early in the morning, snapped on the lights to her classroom in the science wing, and let out a loud, piercing scream. At first her fellow teachers had ignored her, thinking she'd simply seen another mouse scurrying across the floor. That sight had become rather commonplace with all the construction work going on outside. It was disrupting the habitat of critters big and small and causing them to seek shelter elsewhere.

When Ms. Wratched's fellow teachers finally decided to investigate, they found her standing in the front of the room with a shocked expression, staring at a gaping space on the wall where a flat-screen TV had been. Now all that remained were a few wires dangling forlornly from where the unit had been ripped from the wall.

In addition, at least ten other students had reported their cell phones or iPods stolen in the past few days. In fact, so many were now missing that when a student went to the main office to report a theft, the bored-looking secretary didn't even look up, but simply pointed to a notebook under a cardboard sign that read: HAD SOMETHING STOLEN? LEAVE YOUR INFO HERE.

Now the entire student body was buzzing about whether the thefts were an "inside job" perpetrated by a

York Middle student or students, or whether a nefarious gang of professional thieves had descended on the normally quiet school.

"I'm going with professional thieves," Willie said now, munching on a cookie. "There's too much stuff missing. It can't be just kids."

Connor snorted and shook his head. "Have you been watching that dumb *Ocean's Thirteen* movie again?" he said. "Why would a bunch of slick thieves target our little school? Huh? How much money are they going to get for a computer and a few crappy iPods and cell phones?"

He took an enormous bite of his turkey sandwich and continued. "Even the TV from Ms. Wratched's room would be small change for your average master thief. He's not risking ten years in the slammer just for that."

Now it was Willie's turn to snort. "Oh," he said, "listen to the star of *Criminal Minds*."

"Make fun all you want," Connor said. "But it's true."

Suddenly, they heard a loud "OOOH! OOOH!" from the far end of the table. Everyone turned to find Marty with his hand raised.

"I have a theory, if you'll permit me," Marty said.

Jordy rolled his eyes. "Marty, you don't need permission to speak here," he said. "And you don't have to sound like such a dweeb. Who talks like that? 'If you'll permit me'?"

A week earlier, Cody had finally coaxed Marty into leaving the geek table at the back of the cafeteria and sitting with his Orioles teammates. But Marty still seemed in awe of his surroundings and had only recently worked up enough nerve to join the conversations. Most days he preferred to keep his head down, nibbling like a tiny woodland creature at the weird sandwiches he brought for lunch, including the hummus-and-cream-cheese-and-onion sandwich that was now grossing everyone out.

"Okay," Marty said, looking around and dropping his voice conspiratorially. "I think Connor's right. I think it's someone right here in school. He walks among us. He talks like we do. He knows our every move."

"You make him sound like an alien," Willie muttered.

"Or an angel. Or a demon," Jordy said.

Marty smiled, revealing a pasty brown mouthful of gunk and tiny green clumps stuck to his teeth. The other boys winced. Well, Cody thought, now we know the cream cheese had chives in it.

"Oh, no, my friend," Marty said. "He's not from another world. Far from it. He's a living, breathing York Middle student. He might even be sitting in this cafeteria right now. Not at this, um, particular table, of course."

"Well, that's a relief," Jordy said.

"The point is that it's probably someone we'd never suspect," Marty continued. "Someone who looks totally innocent. Someone like, I don't know, Nicky Evans."

"Nicky Evans stole his own cell phone?" Willie said.

Marty shot him a withering look.

"I'm just using him as an example, Einstein," he continued. "It's someone who doesn't draw attention to himself. But someone who knows where everyone keeps stuff."

Cody finished his lunch and crumpled his brown bag into a ball, staring pensively at Marty. "You keep saying *he*," Cody said. "What if the thief is a girl?"

"Highly unlikely," Marty said. "Girls are more likely to engage in crimes such as shoplifting and things of that nature. Everybody knows that."

"There he goes again," Jordy said. "Sounding like a college professor."

Connor said, "And how would a girl rip that big TV off the wall in Ms. Wratched's room? And carry it away? It must've weighed fifty pounds."

Oh, I know a girl who could do that, Cody thought. She'd probably fly through the air, karate kick it off its bracket, and catch it on the way down.

"Mark my words," said Marty, craning his skinny neck and letting his gaze sweep dramatically from one side of the cafeteria to the other. "The thief walks among us."

"Then I wish the thief would steal that disgusting sandwich of yours," Willie said. "It's making me sick."

Eddie Murray Field was all dressed up for the first game of the play-offs. The green grass was freshly mowed, the infield dirt had been raked, and the batter's boxes and base lines gleamed with a new coat of lime. Fancy red, white, and blue bunting hung from the outfield fences too, just as it did from major league stadiums that hosted the World Series.

At precisely 6:30 p.m., county executive Morris Slaughter picked up a portable microphone and strolled out to home plate to welcome the overflow crowd. Slaughter was resplendent in a dark pin-striped suit, crisp white shirt, and bright pink tie, which matched his complexion, courtesy of a recent weeklong vacation in Aruba.

"Whoa!" Jordy whispered in the Orioles' dugout. "Somebody forgot the sunscreen!"

"The man is a walking ad for skin cancer!" Connor said.

Slaughter smiled, revealing two gleaming rows of even, professionally whitened teeth. He cleared his throat and began. "Ladies and gentlemen, it's a wonderful evening for baseball! And as your two-time county executive, it gives me great pleasure to welcome you to this wonderful facility, for this long-awaited game . . ."

"He makes it sound like the Super Bowl," Willie murmured.

". . . between the Orioles and the Red Sox!" Slaughter concluded with a flourish.

At this, the Orioles looked at each other with puzzled expressions.

"Uh, aren't we playing the Braves?" Willie said.

"Sure looks like them in the other dugout," Jordy said. "Know how I can tell? 'Cause it says B-R-A-V-E-S on their jerseys."

As the rest of the Orioles cracked up, a nervous-looking aide walked up to the beaming county exec and whispered in his ear. Slaughter's smile faded, and he raised his hands to the crowd apologetically.

"Ahem," he said, "of course, I meant the long-awaited game between the Orioles and *Braves*."

This elicited a loud sarcastic cheer from the Braves' dugout as well as from their family and friends in the bleachers, which in turn caused the veteran politician's face to turn from pink to a deep shade of red.

"And now," he went on hurriedly, "if you'd rise and join me in the singing of our national anthem . . ."

The crowd rose, but for maybe fifteen long seconds, there was only silence. County Executive Slaughter stood awkwardly at home plate, his hand over his heart, glancing around to see what the holdup was. His aide looked as if he might faint. The problem was soon diagnosed: the sullen teenager working the sound board forgot to hit the PLAY button. Finally he did, and the first strains of the anthem crackled over the loudspeakers, to everyone's enormous relief.

"Men," Coach said when it was over, "I hope our game goes smoother than the pregame ceremonies."

"There are five-car pileups on the Beltway that go smoother than that," Willie muttered.

Robbie set the Braves down in order in the first inning, showing off a good fastball and changeup. As the Orioles came to bat, Cody noticed that the same pitcher who had smirked at him in the first game was back on the mound for the Braves. The kid's name, Cody had learned, was Logan Morrissey. And Logan had turned out to be an okay kid. He was in Cody's gym class and always picked Cody first when they were choosing up sides.

Today Cody wasn't worried about any of the Braves smirking at him. The teasing had stopped out here, just as it had in school. The reason wasn't hard to figure out: Cody had dropped a few pounds. Oh, no one was ever going to ask him to model tight jeans for Old Navy. But he didn't look like that Terry Forster guy—what did they call him, a big tub of goo?—in his uniform anymore.

But with or without smirking, Logan was throwing just as hard as Robbie, and the game quickly settled into an old-fashioned pitchers' duel. The Orioles managed just two hits over the first five innings: a single up the middle by Dante in the second inning, and a bloop double down the right-field line by Yancy in the third. But the Braves weren't doing much better against Robbie and Mike Cutko, who came on in relief in the fifth inning and continued to shut them out.

Cody was growing increasingly frustrated. He had grounded out to shortstop in the second inning, completely fooled by a Logan changeup. In the fourth inning, trying to get something going for his team, he had swung for the fences, taking such a mighty cut at another changeup that he nearly fell down while lifting a harmless pop-up to the third baseman.

"Hey, Babe Ruth!" Willie said when Cody had returned to the dugout with his head down. "You're swinging out of your shoes!"

As the Orioles came to bat in the bottom of the sixth inning with the score still tied at 0–0, Coach tried to keep their spirits up.

"Murderers' Row was just taking a little siesta, men!" he shouted. "The bats are gonna wake up right now!"

Instead, Murderers' Row kept right on snoozing. But, luckily for the Orioles, they got some major help from the Braves' defense when Robbie led off with a bouncer to second that the second baseman bobbled. Jordy moved him over with a weak ground ball to the first baseman. And Connor followed with an even weaker grounder back to the pitcher, moving Robbie to third.

Two outs, yes, but now there was a runner on third. The Orioles couldn't believe their good fortune.

"It's all that clean living, boys!" Coach shouted from the third-base coaching box. "We haven't even hit the ball out of the infield, and we can win it right now!"

Not only that, but Cody, one of their best hitters, was striding to the plate.

Cody gave his bat a quick pep talk—since Marty had busted him, Cody had gotten good at doing this without moving his lips. As he dug in against the Braves' new pitcher, he kept reminding himself: *No Babe Ruth swings. All we need is a base hit.*

The first pitch was in the dirt for a ball. He swung at the second pitch, a low fastball, and fouled it off. The third pitch was outside.

The count was 2–1. He'll probably come with something right over the plate now, Cody thought. He stepped out and tapped the dirt from his spikes. As the noise from the Orioles' dugout and the stands grew louder and louder, Cody could feel the adrenaline coursing through him. He dug in again and waggled the bat menacingly.

The pitcher peered in for the sign. He nodded and came to the set position, ready to deliver. Cody took a deep breath, waiting, waiting . . .

Suddenly a voice rang out. "TIME!"

It was Marty, coaching at first base. He stood there with his hands raised until the umpire granted him the time-out. Then he motioned for Cody to join him for a conference. Over in the third-base box, Coach stared at Marty as if he'd lost his mind.

Marty met Cody halfway down the line and draped a skinny arm around his teammate's shoulders. "Just hear me out on this, okay?" he said. "Don't go all Mount Vesuvius until I'm finished."

Cody was dumbfounded. "This better be good," he said.

"You should bunt," Marty said quietly.

"Ex-*cuse* me?"

"Bunt," Marty repeated. "B-U-N-T."

"I know how to spell it," Cody said. "But why would I do it?" He stared at Marty for a moment with a puzzled frown. Then he said, "Tell me the truth. Are you insane?"

"*Au contraire*," Marty said calmly. "Here's why you bunt. Number one, they won't be expecting it from a big kid. Number two, Robbie's pretty fast—he should score easily. Number three, the pitcher doesn't look like a very good fielder, so you'll probably leg it out for a hit. Even with your, um, less-than-blazing speed. No offense."

"Oh, none taken!" Cody snorted. "Why would I be offended?"

"And number four," Marty said, "let's face it, you haven't exactly been knocking down the fences tonight."

Cody couldn't argue with that. But *bunt*? Here? In this situation?

"Trust me, big guy," Marty said, giving him a whack on the butt, big-league style. Then he trotted back to the coach's box with a self-satisfied smile, like someone who had just saved the planet from a deadly disease.

Walking back to the plate, Cody conducted an internal debate with himself. Bunt or swing away? Should I listen to the little geek? Within seconds, he had made up his mind.

He took a couple of mighty practice swings and dug into the batter's box again. As the noise grew once more, the pitcher squinted in for the sign and nodded. But as he rocked back to deliver, Cody suddenly squared around, the bat held loosely in front of him, waist-high. The pitch was low and outside, perfect for what he was about to do. He dropped the barrel of the bat on the ball, pushing it down the first base line. With a little bit of backspin on it, the ball seemed to die perfectly.

As he took off for first, out of the corner of his eye, Cody could see Robbie racing for home. The pitcher and the first baseman both charged the ball. But each hesitated for a split second, thinking the other had it. Finally the first baseman scooped it and made a high, hurried throw to the catcher as Robbie slid across the plate.

"SAFE!" the umpire yelled.

Game over. Final score: 1–0 Orioles. As they raced from their dugout, whooping and cheering, Cody grabbed Marty in a bear hug before the two were mobbed by their teammates.

Suddenly, they felt the presence of someone looming over them.

It was Coach. He didn't look very happy.

"Marty," Coach said as the jubilation quickly subsided, "are you the coach of this team now? Huh? Did I die and leave you in charge?"

Marty froze, eyes wide with alarm. He tried to stammer out a reply. Then Coach's face broke into a big grin, and he clapped Marty on the back, nearly causing him to pitch forward.

"I'm just messing with you, son!" Coach said. "That bunt call was pure genius! That's using your head! That's taking what the other team gives you!"

Marty clutched his chest and pretended to keel over. "You got me good, Coach," he said. "Can a thirteen-year-old have a heart attack?"

Now everyone was laughing and high-fiving. The Orioles

were still undefeated. One more win and they'd play for the championship. And all because of a bunt, Cody thought.

He looked over at Marty, who was now explaining his strategy to his rapt teammates.

Maybe Coach is right, Cody thought. Maybe the little nerd really *is* a genius.

It was a hot, humid Saturday afternoon and Cody and his parents were working in the backyard, planting a bunch of shrubs with funny names that his mom had recently bought at the local nursery.

It wasn't exactly Cody's favorite thing to do on the weekend. Earlier, he had tried to get his mom to go to the Verizon store to replace his cell phone, which had never turned up, despite Coach Mike's assurances. Instead both parents had appeared dressed in old work clothes and muddy boots, lugging a bunch of garden tools and motioning for Cody to follow them.

"I'm doomed," Cody said under his breath as his dad filled him in on the job that needed to be done.

Planting the shrubs turned out to be hard work. They used a pick to soften the ground, but the pick head kept hitting big rocks, creating sparks, and sending an uncomfortable vibration through the handle and up the arms of whoever was using it.

After a half hour, Cody's shoulders ached, and his hands were becoming red and swollen. All three of them were sweating through their shirts.

"I thought they outlawed chain gangs," Cody grumbled.

"No, they're still legal in Maryland," his dad said with a straight face. "I checked the statutes. Keep working."

When they finally took a water break and collapsed in a couple of lawn chairs under an oak tree, Cody said to his dad, "When are you going to investigate the big crime wave at my school?"

Steve Parker grinned and wiped his brow. "That's a matter for the county cops, not us humble city POH-leece."

"It's still going on?" his mom asked.

"Oh, yeah," Cody said. "Somebody stole a violin from the music room yesterday. And money from the student store. They took the whole lockbox. They even stole an Elmo."

Now his dad looked stricken. "They stole the furry little guy from *Sesame Street*?!" he said. He turned to his wife. "Honey, call the FBI! It's the crime of the century! Someone stole Elmo!"

Cody knew his dad was messing with him. And that it could go on for a while.

"Oh, this is big news!" his dad continued, shaking his head. "Elmo abducted! I wonder if they'll have a story about it in *The Baltimore Sun*?"

His mom joined in. "We can only hope Big Bird and Grover and Cookie Monster are safe!"

"Let me know when you're through," Cody said, rolling his eyes.

"Okay, okay," his dad said, throwing up his hands. "Just a little detective humor."

"*Very* little," Cody said. "For your information, an Elmo is this camera thing the teachers use in classrooms to project objects on a screen. It's supposed to be pretty expensive."

"This is how old I am," his mother said. "When I was in school, they used a *projector* to project objects on a screen."

Cody let that one roll by without comment.

"Mrs. McManus, our assistant principal, also said a box of printer cartridges and Ethernet cords was stolen from the storage room," he said.

"Wow," his dad said. "They'll take anything that isn't nailed down." He took a long gulp from his water bottle and wiped his mouth with the end of his sleeve. "What about security cameras?"

"They're all over the school," Cody said. "But mainly in the hallways. The police have checked the tapes too. But apparently all they can see are shadows."

"Interesting," his dad said. "Whoever's involved here, they definitely know what they're doing."

Cody nodded.

"And it's probably more than one person," his dad continued. "All these different items that are missing . . . One thief couldn't get around the whole school and steal all that."

Kate Parker looked worried. "I didn't know you were going to such a . . . rough school. When we moved in, the Realtor told me it was the best one in the area."

Cody leaned forward in his lawn chair, opening and closing his sore hands. "York Middle's a good school," he said. "It's just facing some challenges right now."

"Yep," his dad said. "It's hard for schools these days, with all the budget cuts and layoffs. . . ."

"But it's not like things haven't been stolen there before," said Cody, unable to resist telling the juicy story he had heard from Mrs. McManus. "A couple of students were busted a few years ago for passing counterfeit money."

"Counterfeit money?!" his dad said. "You gotta be kidding me."

"Nope," Cody said. "And get this: she said the kids made the money themselves."

"Where'd they get the printing presses and the plates and that stuff?" his mom asked.

"Wow, you *are* old school," Cody said, twisting away to avoid her playful slap. "No, the kids used a PC and a scanner and a printer. But I guess the quality wasn't too good, 'cause they got caught giving fake five-dollar bills to Mrs. Nieves in the cafeteria. And she's legally blind!"

His dad laughed and slapped his thigh. "Speaking of counterfeit, this is absolutely true," he said. "Maybe eight or nine years ago, a woman was busted at a Walmart for trying to buy merchandise with a million-dollar bill. You can Google it."

"A million-dollar bill?!"

"Which, as you know, the U.S. Treasury doesn't even make," his dad continued. "That's why these morons always get caught. You watch. They'll catch whoever's doing the stealing at your school too."

They sat for a few more moments, enjoying the cool shade and the slight breeze that had arisen.

"Okay, buddy," his mom said at last, rising to her feet.

His dad followed suit, draining the last of his water bottle and tossing it on his chair. "Time to get back to work."

Cody groaned and rubbed his sore shoulders. "I was afraid you'd say that."

"Up and at 'em," his dad said. "Oh, and Cody?"

"Yeah?"

"I sure hope they find Elmo. Keep us posted on the little guy, would you?"

"And let us know if anything happens to Bert and Ernie too," his mom added.

With that, his parents dissolved in a fit of laughter before picking up their garden tools.

Cody shook his head and smiled. My folks sure have a strange sense of humor, he thought. Sort of like the coach's. Must be a disease all adults have.

Coach Ray Hammond had no ego. Or so it seemed to the Orioles, and they liked that about him. Unlike some other coaches in the league, Coach didn't act like every game was the seventh game of the World Series and only his managerial genius was keeping his team from a certain loss and utter humiliation. In fact, whenever the parents of the Orioles congratulated him and told him what a great job he was doing, Coach would shake his head and point to the players and say, "Nah, it's not me. They deserve all the credit."

Now, with the Orioles' record at 12–0 and his team one win away from competing for the championship, Coach told them his philosophy: *Please don't let me screw this up.* With the Orioles playing so well, he was determined to keep them loose. Yes, he wanted them to focus on their next play-off game against the Twins and their great pitching. But more than anything, he wanted them to enjoy what they had accomplished to date. And he also wanted them to have fun.

So, when the Orioles gathered for practice on a humid

Wednesday afternoon when there was no school—due to a teachers' conference—Coach greeted them with this announcement: "Men, I know this will break your hearts, but no drills today. Today we're playing an intra-squad game. You guys choose up sides. Make 'em fair. I'll pitch for both teams."

As the Orioles cheered and began talking excitedly about who would be on each team, Coach held up his hand for quiet. "Oh, and one more thing," he said, grinning. "Trash talk is not only encouraged, it's mandatory. Just keep it clean."

What followed was seventy-five minutes of barely controlled chaos. Cody quickly decided it was probably the most fun he'd ever had playing baseball in his whole life. They played with six players on a side, positioned wherever they wanted to position themselves. Coach let the players run their own game. He wouldn't even call balls and strikes, or "safe" or "out" on the bases. The Orioles had to work it out for themselves.

"This is what baseball was like when I was growing up!" Coach shouted at one point.

"That was around when, the Civil War?" Willie yelled. Coach waggled a finger at him and flashed an okay-you-got-me smile.

"Point is," he said, "it was before adults became over-involved and started screwing things up!"

The four-inning game between Willie's Wildmen and Jordy's Jammers was a hoot. Each time a player whiffed on one of Coach's slow, tantalizing curveballs or let a ground ball roll through his legs in the field, he was ragged unmercifully. Yet amid all the hooting and hollering, there were great plays: Connor going deep in the hole at short to backhand a grounder and nip Yancy at first; a diving catch of a sinking line drive by Dante; a soaring home run by Jordy high enough to draw rain.

But the highlight, everyone agreed, was the comical sight of Marty chugging around the bases on a disputed triple—it was later ruled a single and a two-base error by Gabe—before collapsing in an exhausted heap after what was possibly the ugliest slide in the history of organized baseball.

"There are glaciers that travel faster than that boy!" Willie said.

Marty, flopping and gasping in the dirt, responded with a single word: "Oxygen!"

Nobody knew who won the game or what the final score was. And nobody seemed to care, either. When it was over, Coach gathered his still-giddy players in front of the dugout and told them to settle down.

"Uh-oh, fun's over," Marty murmured. "Coach's got his game face on. We could be here a while."

But Coach kept his remarks short and sweet.

"Now it's time to start thinking about the Twins," he said. "They're a good team. Their pitching is excellent. It won't be an easy game. Be here early Friday so we get in some good batting practice and infield."

As the Orioles gathered up their gear and Cody changed out of his spikes, a voice behind him said, "Perfect timing."

It was Jessica. She was wearing her red-and-white soft-ball uniform, with her bat slung over her shoulder and her glove dangling from the knob. Cody grinned and quickly glanced around for Dante. The sight of Cody and Jessica together would probably have the big dude vibrating like a gong. But Dante had already left.

Jessica plopped down on the bench beside Cody, took off her cap, and began fanning herself.

"What are you doing here?" he asked.

"We just finished practice on the other field," Jessica said, breaking into a mischievous smile. "How did I do? Thought you'd never ask. Hit three homers in batting practice. Fielded my position flawlessly, as usual. And catcher, as you know, is only the most critical position in softball. So all in all, I'd say, pretty typical practice for blondie here."

Cody rolled his eyes. One thing was for sure: Jessica was never at a loss for words when she was competing in sports. He could definitely see her becoming a lawyer someday. Possibly by the age of fourteen, if they'd let her take the bar exam.

"Anyway, you're coming with me, Wisconsin Boy," she said now.

He looked up from tying his shoes. "But my mom is picking me—"

"All taken care of," Jessica said. "I called earlier. Both your mom and my mom said we could walk home. Today I'm introducing you to another Maryland culinary tradition."

She glanced up at the broiling sun and began fanning herself even more furiously. "Perfect day for it too," she said, rising to her feet. "You're in for a real treat. Follow me."

Cody slung his equipment bag over his shoulder, and they set off in the direction of town. As they walked, he told Jessica all about the raucous practice the Orioles had just had, and Jessica told him about one of her teammates, Amanda, who'd been hit in the face with a bad-hop ground ball in the middle of their practice.

"She started crying!" Jessica said, shaking her head. "And all the other girls are around her, going 'Awww, poor Amanda, are you okay, babe?' Can you believe that?"

Cody started to answer. Then a tiny alarm bell went off in his head. *Better not say anything. Let's see where this is going.*

"It made me want to puke!" Jessica continued. "So I used that famous line from that old movie. You know the one: 'There's no crying in baseball'? And now all the other girls are like, 'Jessica, how can you say that? Don't you have any feelings? Can't you see she's upset?' Which made me want to puke even more."

Cody thought, I feel sorry for any softball that hits Jessica in the face. She'd probably bite the ball in half and swallow it.

After about ten minutes, they turned a corner and Jessica said, "Ah, here we are." It was a small wooden stand tucked back under a grove of trees, with picnic tables and patio umbrellas out front. A sign in front said: OASIS SNOWBALLS.

"The legendary Baltimore snowballs," Cody said, grinning. "Shaved ice and flavored syrup, right? I've heard a lot about them."

"Prepare to be wowed," Jessica said, pulling a ten-dollar bill from her pocket. "Pick a flavor. My treat."

The list of flavors was endless. Cody finally settled on

black cherry. Jessica ordered something called Skylite, which turned out to be a neon-blue concoction she said tasted like raspberry—well, sort of. They sat in the shade, spooning the icy treats from plastic cups. Cody wondered if he had ever tasted anything so delicious in his life.

If you liked to eat, he thought, there were a lot worse places to live than Maryland.

When they were finished, they tossed their cups in the trash and said good-bye to the teenage girl behind the counter. It was then that something in the strip mall across the street caught Cody's eye. A battered green Jeep was pulled all the way around to the side of the parking lot, right up against the woods. The Jeep looked familiar. The rear hatch was open and a half-dozen young men were peering at whatever was inside. Occasionally, they glanced nervously over their shoulders.

The driver's door opened and a dark-haired boy of about eighteen got out. Then another dark-haired boy emerged from the passenger side.

"Hold on a minute," Cody said quietly, his eyes never leaving the Jeep. "I need to check something out."

Jessica stared at Cody as if his head had just exploded.

"You're going *where*?" she said.

"Into the woods," he repeated. "Be back soon."

"Gross!" she said. "You can't wait till you get home?"

Cody smiled and shook his head. "It's not for that," he said. "I have to investigate something. But there's no time to explain."

"Fine," Jessica said. "I'm going with you."

"No," Cody said, throwing down his equipment bag. "You stay here with our stuff. See that Jeep across the street? If it pulls out while I'm gone, write down the license plate number."

Jessica nodded uncertainly. "Ohhh-kay. Write it down with what?"

"Ask the girl at the snowball stand," he shouted over his shoulder. "She's gotta have a pen and paper."

With that he was slipping into the woods and moving south, following the tree line as it crossed the road and circled the parking lot of the strip mall. There was no path, which made for slow going. It was much cooler in there, though, the thick canopy of overhead branches blocking out the sun. Insects buzzed all around him, birds chirped, and occasionally he heard a larger animal, a squirrel, maybe, or a raccoon, scurrying off into the underbrush.

Leaping over a log, he felt something crunch under his sneakers. Looking down, he saw it was an empty beer can. In fact, there were rusty beer cans scattered all over. Someone had apparently thrown a big trash bag full of the things from a passing car, and the bag had ripped. Cody shook his head in disgust.

As he made his way through a thicket, pushing branches aside and stepping over fallen tree limbs, Cody thought about what he had just seen.

Was it the Jeep he thought it was? If so, what were they doing over there so far away from all the stores, behind the Dumpster? And what was so fascinating inside the Jeep?

It all looked very suspicious. A theory was beginning to form in the back of his head. He hoped he was wrong. But he knew it was more likely that he was right, a prospect that made him shiver slightly in the cooler air.

It took a good ten minutes for Cody to circle the woods until he was parallel to the parking lot. Finally, he heard voices up ahead and music blaring from a car radio. Quietly, he dropped down and began crawling on his hands and knees toward the edge of the tree line.

Something moved in the leaves to his right. A mouse? A snake? Cody wasn't terrified of snakes like "Mad Max" Wheeler. But he wasn't exactly looking forward to one slithering up for a face-to-face meeting either. What kind of snakes did they have here in Maryland, anyway? Copperheads? Water moccasins? Rattlesnakes? He made a mental note to look it up when he got home.

Or maybe it was better to say *if* he got home. Because if his theory was right and the guys around the Jeep caught him snooping, they wouldn't be in a great mood. In fact, they'd probably want to use his head for batting practice. The thought had his heart hammering in his chest.

He was only about thirty yards from the Jeep now, atop a steep embankment that dropped down and ended abruptly ten feet above the parking lot. He crawled under a pine tree and peered cautiously out from beneath a bough.

The guys were still there, examining something in the back of the Jeep and talking excitedly among themselves. Cody didn't recognize most of them. But there was no mistaking the two scowling teens leaning on either side of the rear bumper, smoking cigarettes.

It was the Rottweiler Twins. Where was Dante? Cody wondered. Still inside the Jeep?

It was hard to see what the guys were looking at—their backs obscured the view. One of them walked away from the Jeep, slapped hands awkwardly with Nick, and hurried off holding a small cardboard box. Moments later, a second one walked away carrying a plastic grocery bag.

Even this close, Cody could catch only snippets of conversation. The hip-hop tunes blaring from the radio weren't helping matters. Neither was the sound of traffic whizzing by on the road.

It was frustrating not being able to hear them. If only

I could just get a little closer, Cody thought. He crawled slowly in the direction of the scene unfolding below, dragging himself inch by inch, hardly daring to breathe.

Suddenly his elbow banged into something hard. It was a dirty, brown beer bottle. He froze as the bottle began to roll down the embankment. It gathered momentum and kept rolling and rolling, seemingly in slow motion. As Cody watched in horror, it reached the edge and seemed to flip in the air, like one of those Olympic ski jumpers doing a somersault.

Then it dropped straight down and shattered on the asphalt with a loud *BANG!*

"What was that?!" someone yelled. Cody was already up and running, crashing back into the woods like a startled deer.

From somewhere behind him, he heard car doors slam and an engine roar to life, followed by the squealing of tires. Were they trying to cut him off, up near the road where the woods narrowed? He ran even faster now, kicking up clumps of dirt and leaping over logs as branches slapped him in the face.

It seemed to take forever, but finally he spotted the snowball stand through the trees and veered to his right, almost running smack into a security fence. Just as he neared the clearing, his sneaker caught on a root and he went flying, landing face-first in the dirt, inches from a picnic table.

When he turned over, Jessica was looking down at him, waving a piece of paper. "I got the license plate number!" she said triumphantly.

"C'mon!" Cody said, scrambling to his feet and grabbing his bag. "Let's get out of here!"

He took off on a dead run and Jessica sprinted after him. They were a full four blocks away before Cody finally slowed to catch his breath.

"Dante and the Rottweiler Twins . . ." he gasped, doubling over with his hands on his knees. "Can't be sure . . . Looked like maybe they were selling stuff . . . out of their . . ."

Jessica stared at him wide-eyed.

"Don't know if they saw me . . ." Cody continued, chest heaving.

Jessica kept glancing around, as if afraid that a green Jeep would come barreling around the corner at any minute with a bunch of ticked-off older boys inside.

"What do we do now?" she asked.

"I'm not sure," Cody said. He straightened up and wiped his brow. Then he adjusted his bag and looked nervously over his shoulder. "But I know this much: we're getting as far away as possible."

Kyrie Mayweather was the fastest pitcher in the league. Rumor was he could hit eighty miles per hour on the radar gun, while no one else came even close to seventy. A tall, skinny left-hander with mini dreadlocks, he was warming up for the Twins now, his fastball making the sound of a bullwhip cracking as it smacked into the catcher's mitt. Watching him, the Orioles were trying not to abandon all hope.

"That is one nasty fastball," Willie said, leaning against his bat in the on-deck circle.

"He's got a sick curve too," Jordy said. "The good news is, his dad only lets him throw five or six a game. He's afraid the kid's going to hurt his arm."

"I'm okay with that," said Connor, watching another of Kyrie's warm-up throws rock the catcher on his heels. "Wish his dad would only let him throw underhand."

Coach clapped his hands for attention. "All right, everybody in here," he said. "Enough with the doom and gloom. Sure, they have Kyrie Mayweather. But we have Murderers' Row, remember? We're just as good as . . . uh, Cody?"

Everyone turned to look. Cody sat at the end of the bench staring off into the distance.

"Cody? Care to rejoin the planet?" Coach said. But Cody was still lost in thought. Coach stuck two fingers in his mouth and whistled loudly.

Startled, Cody jumped to his feet.

"Sorry, Coach," he said, his face reddening. "Just thinking about something."

"I see that," Coach said. "You'll have to tell us who the girl is later."

As the rest of the Orioles cracked up, Cody managed a sheepish grin, his face growing even redder.

For one of the few times in his life, he was finding it hard to concentrate on baseball. His head was still spinning from the events of the past forty-eight hours, starting with the strange little drama he'd observed with the Rottweiler Twins and their Jeep—until he turned into a major league klutz and scared everyone off.

On the way home that day, he and Jessica had convinced themselves that they had solved the mystery of the Great York Middle Crime Wave. It was simple: Dante and his brothers were stealing stuff from school and selling it from the back of the Jeep. You didn't have to be Sherlock Holmes to figure it out.

But that night at the dinner table, when he had recounted what he'd seen to his mom and dad, Steve Parker had frowned and held up his hands in the universal signal for *Whoa, not so fast*.

"I agree it seems suspicious," his dad said. "But you didn't get a good look, so you're not exactly sure what those boys were doing. You don't know what was in the back of the Jeep. You're not even sure Vincent and Nick were *selling* anything. You didn't see any money change hands, right?"

His mom nodded and said, "And even if they *were* selling something, it could have been something perfectly legal. They could have been selling, I don't know, their old video games."

Cody rolled his eyes. "No, Mom. Believe me, this wasn't what you'd call a wholesome crowd."

"Or they could have been selling something *illegal*," his dad added, "but not necessarily items stolen from your school." He shot his wife a look before saying, "Could have been drugs. We can't be naive about it. But we just don't know."

Cody leaned forward in his chair. "I just know Dante is up to something. He and his brothers—"

"Dante?" asked his mother. "Was he there too?"

"He must have been sitting in the car," said Cody.

"But you're not sure?" his dad probed. "You didn't see him?"

"No, but—"

"Cody," his mom said, her tone a warning, "are you sure you aren't letting your feelings about Dante color your judgment here?"

Steve Parker nodded in agreement. "You gotta be careful, buddy. These are serious allegations you're making, and you're already in hot water with Dante, for whatever reason. If he knew you were sharing your suspicions with a cop . . . well, it wouldn't exactly win you any points with him."

Cody's mother patted his hand. "Promise me you'll drop this?"

"Mom's right," said his dad. "You need to stay out of it and let the police get to the bottom of what's going on."

Cody had to admit that what his parents had said that night made sense. What did he think he was, some kind of ace detective like his dad?

Yet the scene in the parking lot continued to gnaw at him. And even if Dante wasn't there, Cody couldn't shake the feeling that his sullen teammate was connected to the rash of thefts at York Middle.

There was something else worrying him too. Had the Rottweiler Twins or any of those other older guys seen him when he tore off into the woods? Vincent and Nick had been to a few of Dante's games—they certainly knew who Cody was. If he *had* been spotted, Cody knew it was only a matter of time before a nasty beat down came his way.

On the other hand, Dante had acted no differently toward him yesterday in school. And he hadn't acted any differently today as the Orioles prepared to face the Twins in their second play-off game. If Dante and the Rottweiler Twins were operating some nefarious stolen-property ring, and the brothers had recognized Cody that day, wouldn't he have at least gotten a clue from Dante's body language?

Cody shook his head, trying to push those thoughts aside. With Kyrie on the mound, firing fastballs that looked like missiles as they crossed the plate, he needed all the concentration he could muster.

Despite Coach's pep talk—and the Orioles all agreed it

was one of his better ones, somehow combining a famous general from World War II, the story of "The Little Engine That Could," and the guy who was trapped in that canyon and cut off his own arm to escape—they got off to an ominous start.

Leading off, Willie swung at three straight chest-high heaters. Three straight times he hit nothing but air. As he trudged back to the dugout with his head down, Jordy whispered, "That might have been the quickest at bat in the history of baseball."

As Willie took off his batting helmet and slammed his bat into the bat rack, Marty said, "I don't know, Kyrie doesn't look that fast to me."

Willie made a sound—*ONNNKKK!*—like a game-show buzzer. "WRONG!" he said. "He's even faster than you think. If you wanna catch up to that fastball, my advice is to start swinging now."

Robbie followed with another three-pitch strikeout. Jordy, batting third, at least ran the count to 2–2 before striking out on a big curveball to end the inning.

As Kyrie strutted off the mound, Marty said, "Is it me, or does it look like he's getting tired?"

The rest of the Orioles stared at him and shook their heads. As they grabbed their gloves and took the field, Willie muttered the thought that seemed to be in everyone's mind: "Gonna be a long game if our boy Kyrie keeps throwing like that."

The Twins nicked Robbie for a run in the second inning on two singles and an uncharacteristic error at first by Jordy, who dropped a windblown pop-up down the right-field line. But Kyrie set the Orioles down in order as Connor grounded back to the pitcher, Cody managed a weak line drive to the first baseman, and Dante struck out.

It was still 1–0 Twins in the top of the fourth inning when Coach called them together in the dugout.

"I have a question for all of you," he said somberly. "And I really want you to think about it before answering. Are you ready?"

The Orioles nodded dutifully.

"Okay," Coach said. "My question is this: Have any of you wet your pants yet?"

Now, there were a few nervous chuckles, but they quickly trailed off because Coach seemed dead serious. Usually there was a twinkle in his eyes when he joked with them. But there was none now.

"Men, I know Kyrie throws hard," he continued. "I know he's intimidating. But I also know you're not even giving yourselves a chance. You're all just going up there doing this—"

He pulled the brim of his cap to the side, closed his eyes, and pantomimed a wild, cartoonish home-run swing. It drew a few more jittery chuckles.

"You," he said, stabbing a finger at Willie. "You're the fastest kid in the league. But you're up there swinging out of your shoes like you're A-Rod or Big Papi Ortiz. How about we get someone on base first?

"And you," he said, pointing at Connor. "You might be the best hitter in the league. But you're swinging at every-thing instead of waiting for strikes. How about working the count for once?"

Willie and Connor hung their heads. Cody braced himself. He sensed what was coming next.

"And *you*," Coach said, his finger dancing inches from Cody's nose. "I don't know where your head's at today. But it's a million miles away. You're probably the strongest kid in the league. The way Kyrie's throwing, all you have to do is meet the ball and it'll end up twenty feet over the fence. What happened to that sweet, compact swing? You couldn't hit a beach ball with that long, looping swing you're taking now."

Cody grimaced and looked down at his shoes. Now the umpire was motioning impatiently for an Orioles' batter to step up to the plate, so Coach wrapped it up.

"Look, I believe in you guys," he said, his voice low. "If Kyrie beats you, that's one thing. But don't beat yourselves. Not now. Not with this great season you're having."

With that, he turned on his heels and walked briskly to the third-base coaching box.

End of discussion.

The Orioles were stunned. No one said anything for maybe ten seconds. They had never seen Coach so upset.

"Wake-up call," Jordy said finally.

The rest of the Orioles nodded. Willie pounded the top of his batting helmet with his fist, grabbed his bat, and muttered, "Let's do this."

Suddenly, Marty jumped off the bench.

"Wait!" he said. "Let's try something. It's gonna sound a little crazy. . . ."

Jordy grinned. "A crazy idea?" he said. "From you? Who could imagine that?"

Marty shot a quick look at Cody and continued. "Everyone ask your bat for a little help. I'm serious. Talk to your bat. Right now."

"Ohhhh-kay," Jordy said, taking a couple of steps backward. "Marty, seriously now, what planet are you from?"

Cody could feel his face redden. He stared at Marty and tried to communicate via furious thought waves: *Mention my name and you're a dead man.* But his nerdy little friend kept Cody's secret safe. Not only that, but Marty quickly convinced his teammates that talking to their bats was no stranger than wearing inside-out rally caps for good luck.

Within seconds, every Oriole—even Dante—had grabbed his bat and was pleading with it for a big base hit.

Digging in against Kyrie, Willie crouched so low that the top of his bat seemed even with the catcher's mask. It was such a comical-looking stance, the Orioles had to stifle a few giggles. Kyrie peered at Willie with a puzzled expression. It reminded Cody of the famous story his dad had told about Eddie Gaedel, a dwarf who had once been sent up to bat by a major league team just so he could draw a base on balls with his tiny strike zone.

Willie's strike zone now appeared to be the size of a party napkin. Kyrie's first two pitches sailed over his head. The next two skipped in the dirt. Tossing his bat aside, Willie trotted happily to first base. Kyrie kicked at the dirt in frustration. But in the Orioles' dugout, there was suddenly new life.

"Hey, what's it called when someone actually reaches that white bag out there?" Gabe said. "Oh, yeah, a base runner. It's been so long, I almost forgot."

With a left-hander on the mound, Willie couldn't get much of a lead. The Orioles knew there would be no base-stealing exhibition from their leadoff hitter today. Still, just to have someone on base against Kyrie seemed like a major accomplishment. And when the next batter, Robbie, worked the count to 3–0, the Orioles were up and cheering on the top step of the dugout.

Robbie stepped out of the batter's box while Coach flashed the signs.

"He's letting him swing away!" Marty cried.

Joey took off his cap and smacked him. "Hey, genius, why don't you say it a little louder so their whole team can hear?" he whispered. "Better yet, why don't you just text them?"

As Coach had anticipated, Kyrie took something off his fastball on the next pitch to make sure it was a strike. Actually, he took a lot off. And Robbie turned on it perfectly, stroking a clean single to right field as Willie flew past second base.

Almost as one, the Orioles whooped and pointed at Coach as if to say, "Great call, big man." Coach smiled and pumped his fist. They were back in the game. Runners on first and third. No outs. And the heart of their order due up.

Now Kyrie was pacing the mound, muttering to himself. And as soon as Jordy stepped in against him, the Orioles knew they were looking at a different pitcher.

Suddenly Kyrie's fastball looked very ordinary. Cody had seen it so many times: a pitcher throwing free and easy—and hard—until he got in trouble. Then he'd often tighten up, lose confidence in himself. It could happen even to a terrific pitcher like Kyrie. And pretty soon the kid was a basket case, either overthrowing and sending rockets over the batters' heads and into the backstop, or aiming his pitches like you'd aim a dart at a dartboard.

Kyrie was definitely aiming now.

"Stick a fork in him," Gabe said as the rest of the Orioles nodded. "He's done."

The next batter, Jordy, hit a shot up the middle to tie the score at 1–1. Connor followed with a run-scoring double to right. Frantic to turn things around, Kyrie sailed two wild fastballs over Cody's head, then grooved another turtle-speed pitch that Cody ripped down the left-field line for an RBI single and a 3–1 Orioles lead.

With Dante at the plate, Kyrie was staring with pleading eyes into the Twins' dugout after every pitch, practically begging the coach to take him out of the game. And when Dante singled to put runners on first and third, Kyrie finally got his wish. Even before the Twins' coach reached the mound, Kyrie was sprinting to the dugout like a kid who needed to find a bathroom really fast.

As the Twins' relief pitcher warmed up, Coach called the Orioles together in the dugout.

"It's a shame what happened to Kyrie," he said. "But you pitchers, try to learn from this. You have to trust your stuff. Can't panic and start lobbing the ball the first time something goes wrong."

Compared to Kyrie's heat at the beginning of the game, the new Twins pitcher seemed to be lobbing it in too. The Orioles pushed across four more runs on five hits before Mike Cutko came on in relief of Robbie and threw two scoreless innings to seal the win.

Final score: Orioles 7, Twins 1. As they met on the mound to smack gloves with Mike and exchange fist bumps, the Orioles felt good about themselves. Somehow, they had found a way to beat the best pitcher in the league. Yes, he hadn't been at his best late in the game. But their patience and resourcefulness had something to do with that too. Whatever the case, the Orioles weren't about to give this one back.

"Now it's on to the championship game, men!" Coach boomed. "The mighty Orioles against the mighty White Sox! Two thirteen-and-oh teams going at it for the trophy and an undefeated season! This is the way baseball's meant to be!"

The Orioles were glad to see Coach in a good mood again. They were even happier moments later when he pulled out his wallet and announced that the ice creams at the Snack Shack were on him.

By the time the Orioles were through celebrating and Cody walked up to the parking lot to meet his mom, the sun was setting and the sky was streaked with shades of pink and orange.

Off to his left, he heard the revving of a car engine. Then a familiar-looking green Jeep backed up and drove slowly past him. It was the Rottweiler Twins. Cody spotted Dante in the backseat, leaning forward and talking excitedly with his brothers. Good to see Dante as excited about the big win as everyone else, Cody thought.

But then all three seemed to be pointing in Cody's direction and nodding.

He shivered slightly and quickened his pace. Seconds later, the Jeep roared off, its tires squealing. Cody looked around to see if the Rizzos could possibly have been pointing at someone else. But, with a sinking feeling, he realized the parking lot was all but deserted. Only his mom's car remained, its taillights winking up ahead.

Well, Cody thought, that answers *that* question.

That day at the strip mall when he thought he might have melted back into the woods like some kind of hotshot Army Ranger and no one had seen him?

It looked like he was wrong.

The class was in its usual funk. Ms. Eleanor Wratched's fifth-period science students were less than inspired by the question she had just posed in her familiar nasal monotone: "Who can tell us how igneous rocks are formed?"

It was a hot day and the air conditioner in the corner groaned listlessly, emitting a thin stream of dusty air that did little to cool the room. Cody looked around at his classmates. Each one displayed virtually the same body language: torso slouched low, elbow on desk with chin cupped in one hand, the other hand close by in case a yawn needed to be stifled.

Boring teacher, boring subject, hot stuffy room—to Cody, Ms. Wratched's class was the educational equivalent of anesthesia. Who cared about stupid igneous rocks, anyway?

Apparently, no one. Not a single hand was raised. Even Marty had failed to raise his hand. And Marty, the smartest kid in the class, usually raised his hand for everything, even if Ms. Wratched wondered aloud if the cafeteria was serving tacos.

Gazing at the vast sea of disinterested faces before her, Ms. Wratched sighed and rose from her desk. A stout woman a tad just under five feet tall, she began strolling the aisles, apparently operating on the theory that proximity to her students would jog their memories and thus facilitate the lesson plan.

"Igneous rocks?" she said again. "C'mon, anyone?"

No, no one raised a hand. Cody shot a look at Marty, wondering if he would take one for the class and answer the question. But Marty was examining a paper clip, holding it inches from his face as if he'd never seen anything so fascinating in his life.

"Okay, then," Ms. Wratched said. "Perhaps I have to call on someone."

If this was designed to make the class snap to attention, it failed miserably. If anything, the eyes of all twenty-three students were even more glazed-over than before.

Ms. Wratched stopped abruptly at Dante's desk and pointed a small, chubby finger. "Mr. Rizzo," she said with a thin smile. "Surely you know. Igneous rocks? How they're formed?"

The rest of the class assumed she was being sarcastic. Not once since the beginning of the school year had Dante ever raised his hand to volunteer an answer. And when called upon by the teacher when he *didn't* raise his hand, not once had he given a correct answer.

"Um . . ." Dante said, head down, doodling a picture of Batman in his notebook. Then, looking up, "What kind of rocks did you say?"

"*Igneous*, Mr. Rizzo," Ms. Wratched said in the same

monotone. "That *was* the homework assignment, wasn't it? Igneous rocks?"

"Guess so," Dante mumbled, still scribbling. After another long pause, "Um, I dunno how they're formed."

Ms. Wratched stared at Dante for a moment. Then she shrugged and walked slowly back to her desk.

"Well," she said sadly, opening the textbook, "I guess this will be more of a lecture than the spirited give-and-take discussion I had hoped for."

As his teacher droned on and on about rocks and magma and the upper reaches of the Earth's mantle, Cody gazed out the window at the bright sunshine and found his thoughts drifting.

He was still preoccupied by the slow drive-by Dante and the Rottweiler Twins had done in the parking lot. Obviously they had spotted him snooping at their open-air merchandise booth at the strip mall. The question now was, What were they going to do about it? And would it ultimately involve him bleeding in any way?

At the Orioles' practice two days earlier, Cody had been on full alert from the moment his mom dropped him off until she picked him up that evening. Same thing at school: as soon as he got off the bus, his head would start swiveling in all directions, doing what his dad always referred to as a "threat assessment."

Yet nothing had happened. Today, though, Cody had noticed that Dante seemed fidgety, his legs jiggling up and down from the time he sat in his seat. Seeing Dante like this was actually making Cody nervous, and the more he thought about the whole situation, the more he—

Suddenly he was aware of an awful silence in the room. Ms. Wratched's droning had stopped. He thought he heard his name. Snapping his head around, he saw the rest of the kids staring at him.

"Mr. Parker?" Ms. Wratched repeated. "We were going over the depth at which magma is produced. But perhaps you'd care to tell us what you find so fascinating outside the window? Is it the green grass growing? Or the flight of a particularly energetic bumblebee?"

Cody heard a few nervous giggles. He tried desperately to kick-start his brain.

"The, um, the depth at which, uh, magma is produced?" he stammered.

"Yes, that is the topic," Ms. Wratched said.

Finally, it came to him. "Well, that's easy," he said. "It's fifty to two hundred kilometers."

Ms. Wratched could not have appeared more shocked if a total eclipse of the sun had just occurred.

"Very good, Mr. Parker," she said at last. "And of course you have your schematic diagram of how lava reaches the surface of the Earth, because that was last night's homework assignment. Perhaps you'd show that to us now?"

Cody grinned. Yes, he could do that too. He reached down for his binder and fumbled through a pile of papers. Something popped out of the side pocket and clattered to the floor.

The entire classroom stopped still. All eyes were on the thin, pink-and-silver object now resting in the middle of the aisle.

Cody stared at it too. It was a cell phone. But not one he had ever seen before.

"Hey, that's *my* cell!" a girl said.

Looking up, Cody saw Dante tapping his desk with his pencil and looking up at the ceiling. Geez, Cody thought. He's acting so nonchalant, he's practically whistling!

"Mr. Parker," Ms. Wratched said in an icy voice, "would you be good enough to retrieve that device? And follow me to the principal's office?"

Principal Richard Stubbins examined the cell phone in front of him. Must be a big fan of TV detective dramas, Cody thought, rolling his eyes. He watched with amazement as Mr. Stubbins, perched behind his huge shiny desk, poked cautiously at the phone with his pen, apparently not daring to touch it in case the police needed to dust it for fingerprints later.

"I didn't do it," Cody said quietly.

He sat across from the principal, sunk into a soft oversized chair that felt as if it were swallowing him. Watching Mr. Stubbins take such pains to avoid touching the phone, Cody felt compelled to add, "You know I just handed it to Ms. Wratched, right? So naturally it has my fingerprints on it."

Mr. Stubbins looked up sheepishly and stopped jabbing at the phone. Now he began thumbing through a stack of papers, eventually murmuring, "Ah, here it is."

Waving the paper, he said, "This cell phone belongs to Amanda Wilson, an eighth-grader whom I believe is in several of your classes. It was reported stolen two weeks ago. From her locker."

Now he peered over his reading glasses at Cody. The only sound in the office was the soft *tick-tick-tick* of the wall clock.

"I didn't do it," Cody said again. "I've never seen that cell before. Someone put it in my binder."

Mr. Stubbins frowned and poked at the cell phone again, as if searching for more clues. Cody watched him and thought, Too much *CSI: Miami*. Way too much.

"Someone put it in your binder," the principal repeated. "Why would someone do that?"

"I don't know!" Cody said. "To make it seem like I'm the thief, I guess. The one who's been stealing all the stuff here in school."

"I see," Mr. Stubbins said. He stood and began pacing back and forth behind his desk.

Cody mulled over whether to tell the principal his theory about the Rizzos. But his head was already buzzing from everything that had happened, and he knew he wasn't thinking too clearly. He rubbed his hands nervously on his jeans and kept quiet.

"There are certain specific procedures that must be followed in all cases of theft here at York Middle," Mr. Stubbins said. He stopped pacing and whirled around. "Forgive me. In all *alleged* cases of theft."

Cody gulped. If that's supposed to make me feel better, he thought, it's not working.

"Naturally," Mr. Stubbins continued, "we will now conduct our own in-school investigation into this matter. This generally takes two or three days. And I must warn you: if the circumstances warrant it and the police are called in, the student faces suspension and perhaps even expulsion from the school."

Cody groaned and slumped even lower in his chair. Suddenly, he was feeling sick to his stomach. He wished he were back in Milwaukee. At least there they knew him well enough never to suspect him of stealing.

"I'm sorry," Mr. Stubbins said, not unkindly. He looked at his watch and said, "It's almost time for the final bell. Go on home. I'll call your parents and let them know what's going on."

Cody stood and blinked back tears. Luckily, there was no one in the hallway as he made his way to his locker for his backpack. And by the time the bell rang and the halls were again teeming with students, he was already making his way out to the bus.

Jessica was at karate class again, so Cody sat by himself, staring out the window on the ride home. When he walked in the door, a note on the kitchen counter said his mom was at a client's house for her home-decorating business and would be home later.

As he'd done on so many other occasions when he was feeling down, Cody grabbed his glove and a ball and headed out to the bounce-back net in his backyard.

For a solid forty-five minutes, he fired ball after ball at the net from twenty feet away. Throw, catch, throw, catch—somehow he found the numbing repetition to be soothing. Best of all, the whole ritual helped him think.

And he had a lot to think about.

In addition to feeling sorry for himself over being unfairly blamed for something he didn't do, Cody felt terrible for his parents. Oh, they would support him—they knew he had nothing to do with this. But how embarrassing would all this be for them? Cody had never been in trouble before—ever. Now he was being linked to a rash of school thefts so brazen they had even been reported on two different occasions in *The Baltimore Sun*!

Also, a suspension would mean he'd have to miss the Orioles' championship game against the White Sox on Friday. Everyone knew the rule: no school, no baseball. It was as simple as that. Here they were, poised on the brink of a golden season, needing only one more win to go undefeated and cap one of the best Dulaney Babe Ruth League seasons ever. The idea that he would miss it was unthinkable. No way, Cody thought. *No way.*

Finally, there was this: by tomorrow the whole school would be buzzing about what had happened in Ms. Wratched's class. Except by the time the rumor mill was through, Cody wouldn't just be linked to a lone cell phone skidding like a hockey puck across the classroom floor. No, it would be assumed that his locker was a vast repository of stolen iPods, laptops, and cell phones that he was peddling to thugs and hoodlums all over town. *Psst! Looking for a flat-screen TV, cheap? Go see my man Parker over there. He'll take care of you.*

Within twenty-four hours he'd be known all over York Middle as Cody Parker, thief. Tears welled in his eyes again at the thought. Cody was pretty sure his good buds on the Orioles—Willie and Jordy and Connor, and especially Marty—wouldn't believe the rumors. Jessica certainly wouldn't. And Coach probably wouldn't, either. But it made him sick to think the rest of the school would soon be talking about him as if he were some low-life criminal no one could ever trust again.

Around five o'clock, he heard his dad's car pull into the driveway. A minute or two later, Steve Parker came out to the bounce-back net and gave Cody a big hug.

"Mr. Stubbins reached me at the office," he said. He dropped wearily onto a patio chair, motioning for Cody to sit too. "Now tell me exactly what happened."

Cody recounted everything that had happened in Ms. Wratched's class as well as his conversation with Mr. Stubbins. His dad nodded and occasionally interrupted to ask questions.

When he was through, his dad leaned over and gave him another long hug.

"I know this is hard on you," he said gently.

Cody looked down. He couldn't say anything, for fear that he'd start sobbing and not be able to stop.

"Someone definitely set you up," his dad continued. "And I'm pretty sure we know who it was. No matter how cool he acted when that cell popped out."

Cody nodded and wiped his eyes with the back of his hand.

"Your mother and I are meeting with Mr. Stubbins tomorrow," his dad said, patting his shoulder. "Don't worry. We'll get this straightened out."

But Cody couldn't stop worrying. Even after his dad went inside to start dinner, Cody stayed outside, firing one ball after another at the bounce-back net as the cool of evening settled in.

Throw, catch, throw, catch . . .

Ten minutes later, he arrived at a decision. No way was he going to stand idly by and let them suspend him for something he didn't do. No way was he going to miss the biggest game of the Orioles' season. In the dim recesses of his feverish, overworked brain, an idea was beginning to form.

But to pull it off, he needed someone he could trust. Jessica? No. The more he thought about it, the more he knew it would have to be someone completely objective. Someone with no dog in this fight.

By the time he went back inside, he knew what he was going to do.

As his father rattled around in the kitchen with his pots and pans, Cody quickly went on the computer to look up a phone number.

He picked up the phone and took a deep breath.

Then he began to dial.

26

Cody began his stakeout the next morning outside the entrance to the York Middle gym, next to the gleaming trophy case that proclaimed the excellence of the school's students in both academics and athletics.

The bell for third period had rung moments earlier, and now the hallways were deserted. As he waited, his eyes came to rest on a big wall display proclaiming, PHYSICAL FITNESS: IT'S FOR EVERYONE! Cody grunted with amusement, seeing as how he was missing his own gym class right now.

He was amazed at how calm he felt. Just a month ago, his palms would have been sweaty and his heart would have been pounding just *thinking* about what he planned to do. But not now. Now he was too angry to be afraid. Too angry even to be nervous, for that matter.

He glanced at the clock on the wall: 10:04. The boy is late as always, Cody thought. But he'll be here any minute. Heck, he loves gym. After all, that's where he does some of his best work—well, at least in the locker room.

From somewhere down the corridor, Cody heard the

faint sound of footsteps. It was him, he could tell right away. There was something distinctive about the sound of Timberland boots shuffling along the tile floor, as if the wearer couldn't be bothered with actually picking up each foot and placing it in front of the other, the way most people walked.

The footsteps drew closer and closer. Cody tossed his backpack into one of the two alcoves that flanked the gym doors and quickly rehearsed what he was about to say.

A solitary figure dressed in a flannel shirt and jeans turned the corner.

There he was: Dante Rizzo.

His eyes widened when he saw Cody.

"Parker! What are you doing here?" he said. For an instant, he seemed wary. Then he said, "I'm surprised they even let you in school after what you did."

"We need to talk," Cody said quietly.

He could see from Dante's demeanor that the big guy was no longer nervous around him. Guess the effects of acting like you're crazy last only so long on bullies, Cody thought. Or maybe Dante figures I'm already in so much trouble, I wouldn't dare start anything here.

"Nuthin' to talk about," Dante said. "Shouldn't take things that don't belong to you, Parker. Didn't your mama ever teach you that?"

Cody pointed at him and said, "You put that cell phone in my binder."

"I don't know what you're talking about," Dante said. He reached for the locker room door, but Cody stepped in front of him.

"You know *exactly* what I'm talking about," Cody said sharply.

Dante took a step back, surprised by Cody's tone. But his trademark sneer returned quickly.

"I'd love to continue this conversation," Dante said, "but just because you're blowing off gym class doesn't mean an honor student like myself can."

Now Cody stepped forward until he was inches from Dante's face.

"I just want you to admit it, that's all," Cody said, his voice rising. "I want you to admit that you tried to frame me. And that you've been stealing stuff from school. And giving it to your brothers to sell."

Dante glanced around quickly, but the hall was deserted. From inside the gym, they could hear the sounds of sneakers squeaking on the hardwood floors and basketballs bouncing off rims.

"That's some imagination you've got, Parker," Dante said. He folded his arms across his chest and smiled defiantly.

"It's not my imagination," Cody said. "I saw your brothers selling stuff from their Jeep. And they saw me too. So you put that phone in my binder to make people think I'm the one doing all the stealing."

Dante clapped sarcastically. "You got it all figured out, huh?" he said. "You're a regular Sherlock Holmes, aren't you?"

"I want to hear you admit it," he said, poking a finger in Dante's chest. "I want to hear you say I'm right."

Dante slapped Cody's finger away from his chest. His

eyes flashed angrily and he pushed Cody into the wall. Cody winced in pain. He could feel panic rising in his throat. Uh-oh, he thought. Now what do I do?

They heard the sound of running in the hallway. Seconds later, Jordy, Willie, and Connor came careening around the corner.

It was hard to say who was more shocked, Cody or Dante.

"Is there a problem here?" Willie said as the three boys came to a stop and glared at Dante.

Cody breathed a sigh of relief and tried to stop the shaking in his legs. Quickly, he turned back to Dante.

"Admit it!" Cody yelled, poking him again. "Just say you did it!"

Dante looked like a cornered animal. "Leave me alone," he snarled.

"NOT UNTIL YOU SAY IT!"

"You heard the man," said Jordy.

"We're tired of your crap," said Connor. "It's time for you to come clean."

Dante's eyes darted nervously from one boy to another.

"Okay, okay," he said in a low voice. "I put the stupid cell phone on you."

"I knew it!" said Cody. "You've been stealing all this stuff, and you wanted me to go down for it!"

"That's really sick, dude," said Willie.

"Wait a minute," said Dante, holding up his hands. "I didn't steal anything else."

"Yeah, like we're going to believe that," said Jordy.

"Believe whatever you want. I'm outta here."

Dante tried again to pull open the locker room door, but Cody put all his weight against it.

"Why bother pretending anymore?" said Cody. "It's over. We know the truth."

"My guess is he's trying to protect someone. . . ." said Connor.

"Someone named Vincent and Nick, perhaps?" said Jordy.

"Can't exactly blame him," Willie added. "I wouldn't want to be on their bad side."

At this point Cody saw a change come over Dante. He got that haunted look in his eyes that Cody had seen a couple of times before.

"It was them!" Dante hissed. "Not me. I didn't take the stuff, I swear. I just . . ." He gulped, maybe to hold back tears. "My brothers said if anyone found out, they would mess me up and say *I* did it!"

Now he was breathing hard, almost panting, and his face was going pale. It reminded Cody of how he felt when Dante had him in a stranglehold. This time Dante was doing it to himself.

The boys stood there, not knowing what to do, while Dante bent over for a minute, trying to catch his breath and collect himself.

Finally he straightened up and wiped sweat off his brow with his sleeve. His expression had changed yet again. The sneer was back.

"What difference does it make if I tell you?" he said. "Who's going to believe a bunch of losers like you?"

Cody stared at him for several seconds. Then he looked

off to his left and said softly, "Did you get all that?"

Puzzled, Dante followed Cody's gaze.

He watched as a stooped figure wearing gym shorts, a tight T-shirt, and battered Chuck Taylor sneakers stepped out of the alcove.

Dante's jaw dropped. It was Coach Michael T. Lombardi.

"My students always want to know how old I am," Coach Mike said with a sad smile. "I'm seventy-two. But my hearing is still great. And I heard all I needed to hear."

A satellite TV truck was parked at the fence when Cody arrived at Eddie Murray Field for the championship game against the White Sox. And there behind the backstop was a man in a navy-blue blazer, holding a microphone, standing next to a guy with a big camera on his shoulder.

"You gotta be kidding me," Cody said as he joined the rest of the Orioles for warm-ups. He pointed at the news crew. "Is this about the crime wave at York Middle?"

"Nope," said Coach, grinning. "This is about the big game. Channel Thirteen will be showing highlights on the eleven o'clock news. You guys are big-time now. Me, I'm due in makeup in five minutes."

"We'll be on the news? Sweet," Willie said, gazing at the reporter and cameraman. He took off his cap and carefully patted his hair. "I want the cameras to get my best side. Not that I have a bad side, kid as good-looking as me."

Cody shook his head in disbelief. We're definitely not in Milwaukee anymore, he thought as he paired off with Jordy to loosen his arm. Heck, in Milwaukee, it seemed like even the Brewers' highlights didn't make the late news half the time.

Cody was glad the entire Orioles game wasn't being televised, because that would have really slowed things down. You saw it these days whenever youth league tournaments were televised. All of a sudden, every kid was doing his best major league impersonation, tapping the dirt off his spikes with his bat each time he came to the plate, or stepping out of the batter's box on every pitch to tighten his batting gloves.

It was all about getting more face time in front of the TV cameras. And it was amazing how many extra mound conferences there were between pitchers and catchers when a game was televised too.

Looking up in the stands, Cody spotted his mom and dad, who had gotten off work early to see the game. Then he heard "CO-DY! CO-DY!" and saw Jessica and five of her softball teammates sitting in the first row, all of them wearing Orioles caps and smiling and waving.

"Dude, you have *groupies*?!" Marty said, staring at the girls. "That's awesome!"

Cody didn't want to spoil the image by pointing out that one of those groupies, the tall, pretty blonde with blue eyes, could probably put her foot through Marty's sternum with a flying 180-degree dropkick, if you got her mad enough.

The pregame festivities were mercifully brief. The league commissioner read a short proclamation extolling the virtues of youth sports, and a six-piece band from a local drum and bugle corps played a snappy—and off-key—rendition of "The Star-Spangled Banner."

Coach didn't waste any words, either, when he gathered them together before they took the field. "We don't care about TV cameras," he said quietly. "We don't care about highlights at eleven."

At this, Willie looked at Cody and silently mouthed, "We don't?"

"We just want to play our best baseball tonight," Coach continued. "And if we do that?"

He looked around at his players, some of whom were already nodding their heads, knowing where this was going.

"If we do that," Coach continued, "I have no doubt which team is going to win this game. Think of the goal we've had all season. All right, hands in the middle. Now let's go."

Trotting out to third base, Cody thought about how weird it was not to see Dante heading out to left field at the same time. But Dante wouldn't be playing any more ball for the Orioles this season—that much was certain. Not after he and his brothers were arrested. Now it was Marty sprinting out to left, smiling broadly and almost vibrating with excitement over his starting role.

Thinking of the powerful White Sox lineup, Cody said a silent prayer: Please don't let them hit it to Marty. Then he caught himself. What a hypocrite I am, he thought. Didn't I always think the coaches were saying that about me when they stuck me in right field?

He pounded his glove and smiled as Robbie finished his warm-up throws and the umpire cried, "Play ball!"

"Go ahead, hit the ball to Marty," Cody murmured under his breath. "He'll be fine. The little nerd will come through for us. Somehow, he always does—even if it's only with his brain."

Four pitches later, the score was White Sox 2, Orioles 0. The leadoff hitter blasted Robbie's third pitch over the right-field fence. The second batter took Robbie's first pitch and golfed a rainbow shot that cleared the left-field fence by thirty feet. Pacing the mound now, Robbie looked like he was about to throw up.

Coach called time and trudged out to talk to his shaken pitcher. Jordy, Willie, Connor, and Cody joined him.

"Okay, you got that out of your system," Coach said.

"They don't all hit like that, do they?" Robbie said, peering anxiously over his dad's shoulder at the White Sox dugout.

"They do when you lob in belt-high softballs," Coach said. "I think the International Space Station is still tracking that last shot."

Robbie managed a shaky grin.

"I should probably throw a little harder, huh?" he said.

Coach nodded. So did all four Orioles infielders.

"I just have to trust my stuff, right?" Robbie said.

Again, they all nodded.

"Take a deep breath, settle down, right?" Robbie said.

Okay, Cody thought, we're starting to look like five bobbleheads with all this nodding.

Coach gave Robbie an encouraging smack on the butt and went back to the dugout. Returning to third, Cody put a glove over his face to keep from grinning. Robbie was still the only pitcher in the league who could script his own pep talks beforehand.

But as it had so many other times, the pep talk worked. Robbie seemed to settle down immediately. He went back to rearing back and throwing hard, and retired the next three White Sox batters to end the inning.

Unfortunately for the Orioles, Murderers' Row failed to murder anything that the White Sox starter threw for the first two innings. Their pitcher was a tricky right-hander named Bobby Greenwell, with a big, sweeping curveball, and he held the Orioles hitless, although they managed to draw two walks.

Nevertheless, Cody could see there was no panic as the Orioles came up to bat in the third inning, still trailing 2–0. They had been through too much, faced too many good pitchers and hitters all season long, found too many different ways to win, to be intimidated now. When he looked up and down the dugout now, all he saw were guys chomping hard on their bubble gum and sunflower seeds, and yelling encouragement to each other, totally focused on getting some runs.

Best team I ever played for, Cody thought. Whether we win or lose tonight.

On the other hand, the game was almost halfway over. They had to figure out a way to get some hits off Bobby, who would end up looking like a young Cliff Lee on the eleven o'clock news if this kept up.

Suddenly a high-pitched voice in the on-deck circle said, "I got it!"

Everyone turned to look. Marty was rubbing his hands

together and grinning like a mad scientist as he studied Bobby's warm-up tosses. Then Marty pushed his batting helmet low on his head, took one last practice swing, and headed for the batter's box.

"Watch and learn, fellas," he said. "Watch and learn."

It was almost painful to watch the Orioles' skinny number-nine hitter at the plate. Shoulders hunched, head swaying back and forth, jittery feet jiggling, Marty looked like someone trying to stamp out a campfire. As he toed the rubber, Bobby looked in at this pitiful creature and smiled, thinking: fresh meat.

Bobby went into his windup, kicked high with his left leg, and threw another big looping curveball. Then it happened. Marty turned on it perfectly and ripped a clean single to left field. The rest of the Orioles gasped. In the third-base coaching box, Coach looked like he was in shock.

As soon as he crossed the bag at first, Marty called time. Then he strolled nonchalantly to the edge of the Orioles' dugout.

"It's not rocket science," he said to his stunned teammates. "The kid's throwing a serious curveball, right? So all you do is stand way up in the batter's box. That way you're hitting the ball before it has a chance to really break."

The Orioles looked at each other, then back at Marty. It was the first time any of them had seen him hit a ball with authority—ever.

For several seconds, no one spoke.

Finally, in a hushed voice, Willie said, "Are you, like, some kind of wizard?"

"Yeah," Joey said. "Like a baseball Harry Potter?"

Marty grinned and put a bony finger to his temple. "It's the Loopus Factor, boys," he said. "Sometimes it's better than being a wizard."

Then he turned and sauntered back to first base.

Moving to the on-deck circle, Willie shrugged and looked back at his teammates. He knocked the weighted doughnut off his bat and headed to the plate saying, "Might as well try it. What do we have to lose?"

Digging in, Willie stood so far up in the batter's box, it appeared he could shake Bobby's hand. He took a fastball down the middle for strike one. Then he smacked Bobby's second pitch, a slow curveball, into right field for a single, sending Marty to third. The Orioles looked at one another again. Marty Loopus, ace batting instructor—how spooky was that? The next batter, Robbie, grounded out to the pitcher. But Jordy roped another slow curve from Bobby into center field to score Marty and trim the White Sox lead to 2–1.

On the mound, Bobby wore a puzzled look. He kept asking the umpire for a different ball, looking suspiciously at each one as if it were the ball itself that was somehow tipping off his pitches to the Orioles.

"The secret of how to beat the boy is out," Yancy

whispered, "and he doesn't even know it!"

The Orioles continued to tee off on Bobby. Connor followed with another sharp single to center to score Willie and tie the game at 2–2. Now it was the White Sox coach popping out of the dugout to talk to his pitcher and do some damage control. In the Orioles' dugout, Marty sat back on the bench with his arms folded and a knowing smile, holding court like some kind of benevolent, if under-fed, baseball Yoda.

"People make this game more complicated than it has to be," Marty said as Willie and Joey, his new disciples, sat listening with rapt attention.

Now Cody was up, runners on first and second, a chance to break the game wide open. Digging in, he used his left spike to scrape away the lime at the front of the batter's box, so he could stand even closer to Bobby. Sometimes the umpire would yell at you if you did that, but this time he didn't. Only instead of throwing another curve, Bobby started Cody off with a fastball down the middle. And followed that with another fastball, high, to run the count to 1–1.

Right away, Cody knew Bobby was abandoning his curveball for the evening, probably on the advice of his coach. This would be fine if the boy had an overpowering fastball, or a wicked changeup, but he didn't. Which was why Cody was convinced that Bobby was about to throw him the mother of all meatballs, a pitch he could crush into the next area code if he didn't get overanxious.

He didn't have to wait long. Bobby's next pitch came in thigh-high, a sixty-mile-per-hour fastball right over the plate that may as well have come with flashing lights that spelled: THIS IS THE ONE! TAKE IT DEEP! And Cody did. His bat was a blur, his swing a quick, compact stroke right out of a hitting instruction manual. There was a loud *PING!* and then the ball was soaring over the left-field fence for a three-run homer, the left fielder staring at it with his mouth frozen open.

The Orioles' dugout exploded with noise. Just like that, it was 5–2, Orioles. Cody didn't want to show up Bobby on his home-run trot. But he took his time rounding the bases, soaking in the moment. And when he touched the plate, his teammates engulfed him, whooping and pounding him on the batting helmet.

The next two innings seemed to fly by. Coach kept reminding them there was plenty of baseball to be played. He even broke out the corny old adage about not counting your chickens until they hatched. Whatever. Robbie pitched a scoreless fourth inning and Mike Cutko mowed down the White Sox in the fifth, and the excitement in the Orioles' dugout was building steadily.

Now it was the top of the sixth inning. It was all the Orioles could think about as they took the field: three more outs and we're champions. *Undefeated* champions too.

Which was exactly when Mike proceeded to walk the White Sox's leadoff batter on four pitches. Before Coach could leap from the dugout, Willie called time and jogged to the mound. The rest of the infielders joined him. Mike held up a hand as if to say, "I'm fine."

"Don't blow it," Willie said. "If you blow it, I swear to God I'll—"

"That's how you settle him down?!" Jordy said incredulously. "'Don't blow it'?"

Willie shrugged. "I like to come right to the point."

"Leave. You're giving me a headache," Mike said, looking at each of them. "The adrenaline got to me with the first batter, that's all. But I'm okay now."

True to his word, Mike stopped overthrowing and found the strike zone again. But on a 2–2 pitch, the next batter lifted a towering fly ball to left field. As Marty staggered under the ball, the Orioles held their breath. He circled right, then left, then back to the right. Cody felt himself getting dizzy just watching. But finally Marty stuck out his glove and the ball dropped into the webbing with a soft thud. Beaming, he held the glove high in the air for all to see.

One out.

The Orioles couldn't help grinning. Marty acted as if he'd just caught the final out of the World Series. But when Cody looked over at Willie, the little second baseman was tapping his chest in a pitter-patter motion like, "Almost had a heart attack on that one." Cody nodded. His heart had skipped a couple of beats too.

It skipped a few more when the next batter, the kid who had led off the game with a homer off Robbie, singled sharply up the middle, putting runners on first and second and bringing the tying run to the plate. Mike hung his head for a moment as Yancy fired the ball back in.

Jordy shot Willie a warning look that said, *Do not, under any circumstances, go talk to Mike, or I will pound you into the ground.* Willie nodded and murmured, "Okay, okay." But Mike composed himself and threw a nasty changeup on a

2–1 count to the next batter, who hit a harmless bouncer to Jordy at first base.

Two outs.

But they hadn't nailed it down yet. The White Sox had runners on second and third. And their number-two hitter, the kid who had golfed the towering home run in the first inning, was coming to the plate.

Now the noise from the stands was deafening. The White Sox family members and friends were up on their feet, screaming for a miracle. The Orioles supporters were jumping up and down and shrieking for Mike to close it out. Jessica and her friends were cheering so hard their faces were red.

Nope, we're not in Milwaukee anymore, Cody thought, as he pounded his glove and got down in his stance.

Mike toed the rubber and peered in at Joey for the sign. He nodded and came to the stretch. Cody saw the White Sox batter take a deep breath, holding the bat high and waving it in tiny circles.

Now the pitch was on the way, a belt-high fastball that the kid waited on perfectly, hitting a soaring drive into the gap in left-center field. Cody gulped. He watched Marty break to his left as Yancy broke to his right. They were closing in on the ball, Marty with his lumbering gait, Yancy with his smooth strides, but it was hard to tell if either would be able to catch it before it hit the ground and skipped all the way to the fence.

"Please," Cody whispered, "don't let it be Marty." He didn't feel guilty wishing this, either. Marty already had his catch.

The ball seemed to hang in the air forever as both outfielders neared it. Finally, at the last second, Marty peeled off and Yancy lunged, making a terrific backhand grab by the tips of his shoes.

Game over. Final score: Orioles 5, White Sox 2. The Orioles were the undefeated champions of the league.

Now they were sprinting toward the middle of the infield, cheering and flinging their hats in the air. And when they finished jumping on one another and rolling around in the cool grass and hugging Coach, they lifted Marty on their shoulders and paraded him around the bases.

Cody looked up in the stands. There were his mom and dad, clapping wildly and pointing at him and giving him the thumbs-up sign. And there were Jessica and her friends, dancing behind the backstop and screaming his name over and over. Now he felt someone tap him on the shoulder. He turned to see the TV reporter in the navy blazer standing next to him, the cameraman setting up in front of him, the camera's red light winking on.

The reporter stuck the microphone in his face and said in his best reporter baritone, "We're talking with Cody Parker, star of today's 5–2 Orioles win over the White Sox for the Dulaney Babe Ruth League. Cody, you guys just finished a magnificent undefeated season. How does it feel?"

Cody tried not to laugh. It reminded him of all the crazy fake interviews he and Willie had done all season. Only this one was real. For the late news, no less.

"How does it feel?" he repeated.

He looked out at the wild scene around him: a dozen

of his teammates, dirty and sweaty and exhilarated, screaming into the twilight and joyfully parading a skinny, nerdy-looking kid around on their shoulders.

Then he looked into the camera and said, "It feels awesome. Absolutely awesome."

Jessica dribbled to her left, making sure to avoid the potted plants that lined the driveway, and announced, "Turnaround bank shot."

Cody snorted.

"Do I look worried?" he said. "That shot's a piece of cake. In fact, I practically invented it."

Jessica rolled her eyes. With her back to the basket, she spun to her right and put up a twelve-foot jumper that kissed lightly off the backboard and dropped through the rim.

Now she was dancing wildly with her hands thrust triumphantly in the air, shouting, "You know the problem with this game? It's too easy for me! I need to play someone with way more game than you've got, Parker."

Cody shook his head in mock disgust and retrieved the basketball. It was a glorious Saturday afternoon, the sky so blue it hurt his eyes. But what was really hurting him now was that he was about to lose at H-O-R-S-E to Jessica again. Even worse, he was getting out–trash-talked too.

"You already know I'm a baseball superstar—on an

undefeated team, I might add," he said, dribbling out to take the shot. "Now you'll see I'm destined for the NBA too."

He pivoted to his right, leaped, and released the ball in textbook fashion, high off his fingertips. Then he watched in horror as it missed the backboard completely and bounced harmlessly into the hedge as Jessica cackled.

"Yeah, you're destined for the NBA," she said. "Except in your case, it stands for Nothing But Air. That's your third loss this week."

Cody pretended to lurch over to the lawn and collapse in sorrow. Jessica grinned and ran inside, returning with two cold bottles of water.

"That was some game last night," she said, plopping down next to him. "But what do you think will to happen to Dante? That's all anyone's talking about."

"Hard to tell," Cody said. "But he's in big trouble, even if what he says is true, that his brothers did all the stealing."

"Do you believe him?" Jessica asked.

Cody shrugged and took a sip of water.

"I'm not sure," he said. "The Rottweiler Twins were definitely running the show, but he was an accessory at least. My dad talked to the county police. They think when I saw them selling stuff out of the Jeep, Dante's brothers told him to plant that cell phone on me. It was a pretty stupid move. But my dad says that's how most bad guys get tripped up. They do something stupid."

Jessica shook her head softly and let out a low whistle.

"I felt terrible for you that day when the phone popped out of your binder," she said. "Everyone in school was whispering about it."

Cody wore a pained expression and rubbed the cool bottle across his sweaty forehead.

"Mr. Stubbins says they're going to make an announcement and run an article in the school paper saying I had nothing to do with the thefts," he said.

Jessica reached over and punched him playfully on the shoulder.

"First the evening news, then the front page. Such a media star."

Cody grinned and pretended to pose for the TV cameras, just as he had the night before, the best night of his life.

"But here's what I really want to know," Jessica said. "How in the world did you get Coach Mike to eavesdrop when you confronted Dante?"

"Easy," Cody said. "I just called and explained my plan. I knew Mr. Stubbins would never believe a kid. Coach Mike agreed to help right away. He kept saying, 'Chief, you're no thief. I've been on this earth long enough to be a pretty good judge of character. And you're no thief.'"

Jessica nodded. "What a great guy. Saved your butt, that's for sure."

"Yep," Cody said. "So did the guys—Willie, Connor, and Jordy. They showed up just in time."

"Before Dante could pound you like . . ."

". . . a bad piece of meat," they said together, then cracked up.

"For a kid who's only been here a few months," Jessica said, "you sure have great friends."

"And you're one of them," Cody said, "Karate Girl."

"Aw, you say that to all the girls," Jessica said with a smile.

"Only girls who can beat my butt!" Cody said, jumping up quickly to avoid another punch.

He ran over to the driveway and picked up the basketball. "But now it's time for me to beat yours!"

He dribbled smoothly between his legs and launched into a courtside announcer's play-by-play: "Tie score, five seconds left . . . Parker has the ball in the corner . . . He spins and puts up a twenty-footer with a defender draped all over him . . . *Swish!*"

Jessica rolled her eyes and rose to her feet. She drained the last of her water bottle, retrieved the ball, and put up a long jump shot from the top of the key.

"Keep dreaming, Wisconsin Boy," she said. "That's what you do best."

If you enjoyed this book, look for

a novel by

CAL RIPKEN, JR.

with Kevin Cowherd

Robbie Hammond stared in at the batter and tried to look intimidating. I need to work on my game face, he thought. Hitters don't dig in against a pitcher with a good game face. Mine is lame. When I try to scowl, I look like a kid who needs to find a bathroom in a hurry.

He vowed to practice in front of the mirror when he got home, if his little sister wasn't around to watch. It was hard to concentrate with Ashley cackling and shouting, "Mom, you gotta see this!"

Robbie got the sign from his catcher, Joey Zinno, and nodded. He went into his windup, kicked, and fired. The pitch was low and outside, but the Tigers batter swung anyway and missed for strike one.

"Yes!" Joey shouted, pointing at Robbie before whipping the ball back. "Now you're dealing!"

Robbie exhaled slowly. Maybe that last pitch wasn't a thing of beauty, he thought. It didn't exactly split the plate. But it was the best one he'd thrown all day, which wasn't saying much, seeing as how the Orioles were getting their butts kicked—again.

He glanced at the scoreboard behind the center field fence: Tigers 5, Orioles 0. And it was only the fourth inning, meaning there was still plenty of time for further disaster. Gazing at the stands, Robbie saw that the Orioles' cheering section wasn't exactly riveted by the action on the field, either. Two dads were talking on their cell phones. Another was pecking away at his laptop. One mom had her head buried in a book.

Even a couple of dogs tied to the fence looked bored. That's how bad we are, Robbie thought. We can even make pets yawn.

Still, as he wiped the perspiration from his brow, Robbie permitted himself a thin smile. At least he hadn't given in to the batter. He'd gone after him, challenged him with his best pitch. He hadn't walked him, the way he had with four other batters so far.

Then he heard it.

"BEND YOUR KNEES! FOLLOW THROUGH!"

There it was again. The same voice he'd been hearing since the season started two weeks ago—an annoying fog-horn that conveyed more than a hint of impatience. If the voice had belonged to a kid, Robbie would've wanted to gag him and shove him into a closet.

The problem was, the voice belonged to his dad.

Robbie glanced over at the Orioles dugout. Ray Hammond was perched on the top step in his usual pose: shoulders hunched, hands jammed into the pockets of his blue Windbreaker, rocking back and forth on his heels. A thick man with a buzz cut under his O's cap, he chomped furiously on a wad of gum the size of a golf ball.

Watching him, Robbie was glad his dad hadn't discovered the joys of chewing sunflower seeds. The man would be spraying them like machine-gun fire about now.

"CONCENTRATE! PUT THIS GUY AWAY!"

Robbie sighed. Give it a rest, Dad, he thought. Let me at least enjoy this rare moment of triumph before I uncork one that sails over the backstop this time.

But his dad wasn't about to stop yapping, Robbie knew.

No, as the new coach of the Orioles, his dad was a nervous wreck. Outwardly, Ray Hammond could fool you. As a Baltimore cop, he projected an air of calmness and authority. And why not? In his sixteen-year career, he'd been decorated numerous times for coolness and bravery in the line of duty.

Just a few months ago, he had answered a call about a domestic dispute and stood in a kitchen across from a distraught man waving a knife. It took over an hour, but eventually Robbie's dad talked the guy into putting down the knife and surrendering. For that, Sgt. Hammond was awarded the Bronze Star, one of the police department's highest honors.

No, there wasn't much that seemed to rattle Ray Hammond—until he took over the Orioles. Here he was less certain of himself, Robbie knew, still finding his way as a rookie coach. And it didn't help that his kid, supposedly the best pitcher on the team, couldn't find the strike zone with a GPS. Or that the Orioles weren't hitting, either, and kept discovering new and innovative ways to lose.

Maybe the rest of the Orioles couldn't tell, but Robbie

knew his dad was stressing in his new role. And one way Coach Hammond dealt with the stress was to bark nonstop advice to his players, in a voice you could hear in Canada.

Coach Motormouth, some of the kids called him when they thought Robbie couldn't hear them. But Robbie heard everything—everything his dad said, and everything his teammates said, too. Which was part of the problem.

"JUST RELAX OUT THERE!"

Oh, that's helpful, Robbie thought. Telling a pitcher who's wild and down 5–0 to relax. A little late for that, isn't it?

Besides, if you *yelled* at someone to relax, didn't it have the opposite effect?

Wouldn't it be better to use a soothing voice—your indoor voice—to calm your rattled pitcher?

No wonder baseball wasn't nearly as much fun this season. Even though he was short for his age, with stubby arms and legs that he feared made him look like SpongeBob, Robbie had always been the best pitcher at every level he played. "You got a live arm, son," his coaches had always said.

At the prestigious Brooks Robinson Camp last summer, he had mowed down one batter after another in the intra-squad games. Brooks Robinson himself, the great Hall of Fame third baseman, had watched from the sidelines and said to one of the coaches, "The boy sure has some giddyup on that fastball."

But that was then.

That was before *it* happened. The thing with Stevie Altman.

Oh, Robbie still had plenty of—what was it again?—giddyup on his pitches. He still threw harder than anyone else in the league. But lately, more often than not, he had no idea where the ball was going when it left his hand.

And now that the Orioles had lost their first six games of the season, his dad was barking at him a lot. Which didn't seem to happen to any of the other Orioles, Robbie noticed.

Now the Tigers batter dug in again. But this time he was crowding the plate, hunched over the inside corner as he waved his bat menacingly in the air.

Seeing this, Robbie froze. Shouldn't the kid step back a little? Wouldn't that be the smart thing to do? Shouldn't he tuck that elbow in so he doesn't—?

"Time!" a voice behind him yelled. Willie Pitts, the Orioles' speedy second baseman, trotted to the mound. He was joined by Connor Sullivan, the big shortstop, and Jordy Marsh, the first baseman.

None of them seemed happy.

Great, Robbie thought. More teammates thrilled with my performance.

"Dude," Willie said sternly, "you're thinking too much."

Robbie nodded sheepishly. "Yeah," he said. "I tend to do that."

"Don't!" Connor said. "Just throw the ball over the plate."

"Yeah, try that," Willie said. "By the way, the plate is that white thing up there. In between the batter's boxes."

"The thing the ump keeps dusting off," Jordy added helpfully.

With that the three looked at one another, rolled their

eyes, and trotted back to their positions.

"Thanks," Robbie murmured. "I feel much better now."

Actually, what he felt was a familiar tightening in his stomach, something that seemed to happen a lot lately when he pitched.

Okay, no thinking, he told himself. Just throw it.

Robbie got the sign from Joey again, wound up, and fired a fastball. It skipped in the dirt. Ball one. The next pitch, another fastball, was high. Ball two. Robbie could see the kid at the plate wasn't going to help, either.

No, the kid was no dummy. He had learned his lesson. He wasn't swinging at any more junk out of the strike zone. Instead he stood there like a statue, bat on his shoulder, as Robbie skipped two more pitches in the dirt and the umpire cried, "Ball four!"

With a smirk the kid tossed his bat aside and trotted down to first base.

The rest of the inning seemed to take forever.

Robbie walked the next batter on five pitches. He walked the batter after that on six pitches. Bases loaded. He was so nervous now, he was almost nauseated.

Oh, God, he thought, please don't let me hurl, too. I'm embarrassed enough without spewing in front of all these people.

But for the first time all game, the Orioles caught a break.

The next Tigers batter, a hulking kid named Ramon who Robbie recognized from gym class, swung at an outside pitch and looped a weak flare over second base. Willie and Yancy Arroyo, the Orioles center fielder, both gave chase.

For an instant, the ball looked like trouble. But Yancy called off Willie and made a running one-handed catch at the last minute for the third out.

Robbie was never happier to get off the mound. Mike Cutko was scheduled to pitch the last two innings for the Orioles, which was fine with Robbie. He was done for the day—in more ways than one.

Oh, he was *so-o-o* done.

As he neared the dugout, his dad gave him a high five and said, "Way to get out of that jam." But Robbie knew his dad was just trying to be encouraging. Or maybe he felt guilty about riding his kid so hard.

Whatever, Robbie thought, the drive home should be fun. He pictured his dad with one meaty hand draped over the steering wheel, quiet and unsmiling, worried about whether he was doing a crappy job coaching the Orioles and wondering why his kid was struggling so much with his control.

Taking a long swig from his water bottle, Robbie was struck by another thought: I wonder if it's too late to go out for lacrosse?

Robbie was slumped on the couch watching TV when he felt something bounce off the top of his head—*Boink! Boink!* He pretended to ignore it. Casually he reached for the remote.

Boink! Boink! There it was again. Robbie sighed. She won't go away, he thought. She never goes away. I know exactly what she wants, too.

Boink! Boink! He whipped his head around. Sure enough, there was his mom, smiling and holding out a Ping-Pong ball and two paddles as if they were weapons for a duel.

"You want to get schooled again?" she said. "Huh? Because I'll beat you like a rented mule."

Despite his lousy mood, Robbie couldn't help grinning. He had to give her credit: his mom was the best trash-talker in the whole world—better than any kid Robbie knew. Better than most pro athletes, for that matter.

Other kids' moms were friendly and talkative, sure. But there was no one like Mary Hammond. "Loud and proud," was how his dad described her. And she was wickedly funny when she trash-talked, too. Whenever Robbie's friends came over, she'd challenge them to one-on-one basketball in the driveway, or Wii games, or Monopoly—anything you could compete in. Most of the time his friends would be laughing so hard at her nonstop chatter that they could barely concentrate.

"You try being married to a cop and being Little Miss Demure," his mom once said of her personality. "Doesn't work. You'd get squashed like a bug."

His mom was no bug. She'd been a terrific athlete at the University of Maryland, a star second baseman on the softball team, and one of the best diggers the volleyball team had ever had. Robbie had seen old grainy video of her laying out for ground balls and throwing herself around the polished volleyball court, and he wondered how she hadn't landed in the emergency room after every game.

She brought the same hard-charging mentality to everything she did in life, including her business: Catering by Mary ("Affordable Elegance for All Occasions"). Robbie feared that his mom's in-your-face attitude may have been what led his twin sister to go to boarding school this year. Though he would never admit it publicly, he missed having Jackie around the house—if only to divert some of his mom's attention.

"What's the matter?" she said, tossing Robbie a paddle. "Afraid to play me?" She flapped her arms as if they were wings. "Chicken? *Bawwk! Bawwk! Bawwk! Bawwk!*"

Robbie shook his head and laughed. "Okay, that does it," he said, clicking off the TV. "Your beat-down will be extra severe this time."

"Oooooh, now he's mad!" his mom said, rumpling his hair playfully. "I'm so sc-a-a-a-red!"

Seconds later they were bounding downstairs to the family room and the dark green Ping-Pong table, gleaming under the harsh fluorescent lighting.

"How was your game last night?" his mom asked as she straightened the net. "Sorry I missed it. Work is nuts. We've got three weddings this weekend. Did the Orioles finally win?"

Robbie groaned inwardly. For the past twenty-four hours he'd been doing everything he could to forget the game. Forget the final score: Tigers 6, Orioles 2. Forget the fact he couldn't hit the ocean—never mind the strike zone—with his pitches. Forget the growing feeling that he was letting down the team, and letting down his dad.

No, he didn't feel like getting into all that now.

"You wanna play, or you wanna talk?" he said, tossing the ball to his mom. "Your serve. Age before beauty."

She narrowed her eyes and pretended to be outraged. "Oh, now it's on!" she said. "You're going down."

But instead, Robbie quickly jumped out to a 10–5 lead. He was a strong all-around player with a good backhand—good enough to win his age-group championship at summer camp. But his mom was amazing at hitting the angles. And she had a tricky spin serve that made the ball shoot wildly off your paddle if you didn't adjust for it.

Plus, Robbie thought, she has that not-so-secret weapon: her mouth.

"You can't hold this lead!" his mom said as they volleyed furiously. "You'll crack like a three-minute egg!"

This time Robbie said nothing. His dad was right: the only way to beat his mom when she started trash-talking was to tune her out. "Pretend it's like static on the car radio," his dad always said. "Just ignore it."

But as the game went on, that was easier said than done. When he was leading 19–15, Robbie sailed two returns long and smacked his thigh in frustration.

"Aacckk!" his mom said, bugging out her eyes and wrapping both hands around her throat. "Is someone starting to choke? Someone need the Heimlich maneuver?"

But on the next point, she was the one who attempted a slam and sent it long. Robbie was at match point: 20–17. He looked at his mom. He could see the perspiration on her forehead. She was breathing hard too.

Again, he knew what was coming.

"Time-out!" she said, as if on cue. She put down her paddle and made a big show of elaborately fixing her ponytail.

"That's so lame, Mom," Robbie said, shaking his head.

"What?" she said innocently. "I'm not allowed to fix my hair?"

"Why don't you put some fresh lipstick on, too?" Robbie said. "Anyway, it won't work. You're just delaying the inevitable."

When she was finally ready, Robbie served. The two volleyed back and forth cautiously for a few seconds, each looking for an opening to attack. Finally, his mom slammed what looked to be a sure backhand winner on an impossible angle mid-table.

Except . . . somehow Robbie got to it.

He lunged to his right and hit an amazing forehand that

struck the top of the net. For an instant, the ball seemed to hover in the air. Then it dinked over for the winning point.

"NO-O-O-O!" his mother wailed, collapsing to the floor and lying facedown on the carpet.

Robbie shrugged and tossed his paddle on the table. "My work here is done," he said. He swiped a hand across his forehead. "Look at that. Didn't even work up a sweat."

"Oh, you're a cruel kid!" his mom said. She got to her feet and pretended to stagger over to the small refrigerator in the corner. She pulled out two water bottles and handed one to Robbie.

"This will haunt me forever," she said, plopping down on the sofa and running the cool bottle across her forehead. "I might never live it down."

Robbie sat and put an arm around her shoulder. "Don't worry," he said. "I won't tell anyone. Except Dad. And Jackie. And Ashley. And all my friends in school. And everyone on the Orioles."

His mom smiled wearily and blew a stray hair out of her face. "Speaking of the Orioles," she said, "tell me about the game."

Robbie frowned and pulled his arm away. "Didn't Dad already tell you about it?"

She turned to look at him. "Maybe I want to hear from the player's perspective."

"It was okay," he said with a shrug.

"That's it? 'Okay'?" his mom said. "Can we have a few details? Like maybe the score? And how my favorite son pitched?"

Robbie took a gulp of water. "Tigers beat us six–two,"

he said quietly. "Your favorite son gave up a lot of walks. Again."

"Yuck!" his mom said.

Robbie nodded. "I didn't even want to pitch. Not the way I've been going. But Dad says I have the best arm in the whole league."

"Not to mention lightning-fast reflexes," she said, gesturing toward the Ping-Pong table. "You just have to hang in there till your confidence comes back."

"You sound just like Dad."

"Who do you think coaches *him*?" his mom asked with a twinkle in her eye. "Seriously, he's right." She patted Robbie's hand. "You'll be back. You were always a great pitcher."

"Thanks for the use of the past tense," Robbie said morosely.

"Oh, you know what I mean," his mom said. She leaned over and kissed his forehead. For a moment, they sat in silence, sipping their water.

Finally his mom cleared her throat and said softly, "Do you still think about it? You know, what happened with Stevie?"

Robbie closed his eyes and felt a shiver go through him.

Do I still think about it?

Only every time I pick up a baseball.

A grand slam series for all readers!

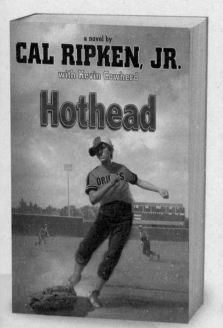

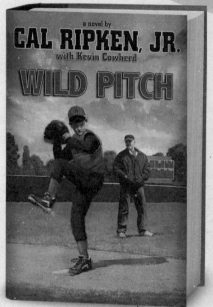

From
CAL RIPKEN, JR.